Lands of Wanderlust Novels by

Paul Yoder

Lords of the Deep Hells Trilogy

Shadow of the Arisen

Lords of the Sands

Heart of the Maiden

Kingdom of Crowns Trilogy

The Rediron Warp

Firebrands

TBA 2024

Lands of Wanderlust

Paul Yoder

The Rediron Warp

Kingdom of Crowns trilogy
Book I

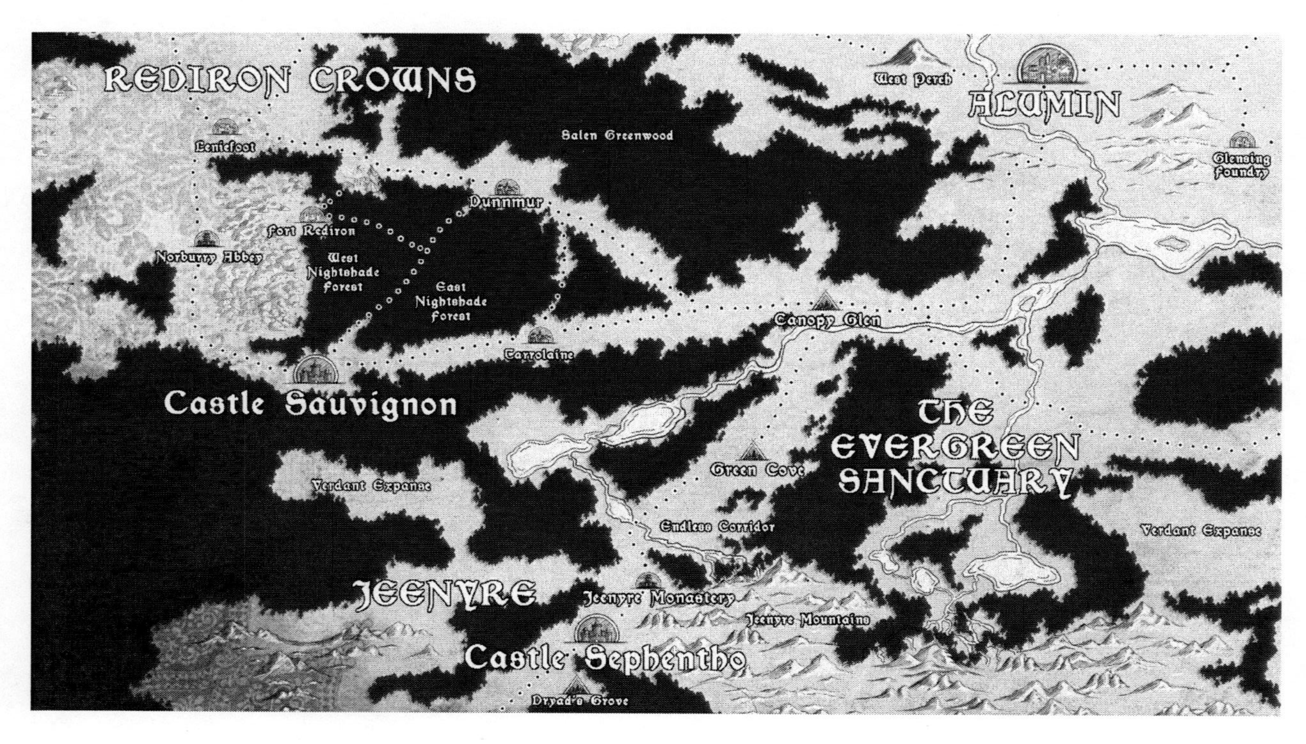
REDIRON CROWNS
Leniefoot
Norburry Abbey
Fort Rediron
West Nightshade Forest
East Nightshade Forest
Dunnmur
Salen Greenwood
Carrolaine
Castle Sauvignon
Verdant Expanse
JEENYRE
Jeenyre Monastery
Jeenyre Mountains
Castle Sephentho
Dryad's Grove
Endless Corridor
Green Cove
Canopy Glen
THE EVERGREEN SANCTUARY
West Perch
ALUMIN
Glensing Foundry
Verdant Expanse

PROLOGUE

That image had burned in his mind all that day. A portly man, possibly a tradesman by the remnants of what was left of his clothes, had been turned inside out and cast to the side of the highway. It must have happened only moments before his arrival at that cursed spot in the road as there had been no flies to the open carrion.

Being a trapper himself, he knew a fresh kill when he saw one, though a slaughter job as the one he had seen there reminded him of no known animal or human's handiwork he could attribute.

"Turned clean inside out," Gerun said, staring blankly into the dark of the heart of trees he was camping in, scratching idly at the flaky patch of skin along his neck.

Shaking out of his remembered vision, he snapped a sappy twig, throwing the rest of the pine kindling in the small fire he had just finished.

Setting about his bags, he pulled out a few parcels and wooden containers. The sun was fast setting, as it always did when he still needed its light in setting up camp. Rarely did it seem to move when he was ready for night to come on.

He had been the only one on the road that day, passing no others for miles. He hadn't expected anything *but* that. The old highway had been bypassed in recent months and few now used it. But for a trapper, it was a perfect, well-paved trail that had become a haven for game once more.

Smoke rose off the open fowl carcass he had snared earlier that day. It was too small to sell at market, but it would be enough to cook up for dinner that night. The chill evening air quickly sapped the recently living pheasant of what residual life-heat the meat still clung to.

Pulling his cast iron skillet from the worn folds of his pack, he coated the surface in a generous amount of ghee, placing the skillet along the rim of the fire where the wood had begun to mature into coals.

A sound in the woods cut through the gentle silence of twilight.

Gerun stood instantly, gripping the handle of his hunting knife along his belt. He peered out into the folds of vegetation surrounding him, but the light of the fire was working against him, making it increasingly difficult to see past his small camp's perimeter. His sore neck tinged, causing him to wince at the muscle spasm.

The sound had been...a voice he thought; but, of man or animal, it came on too suddenly for him to tell.

He had decided to camp quite a ways off the road that night in lieu of the dead man he had happened upon earlier that day, just to be safe in case the culprits had been highway bandits. He was more than far off the highway's path to expect travelers out near his camp, and that, even for a seasoned woodsman like himself, more than disturbed his peace of mind.

He stood still—the only sounds were that of his fire and the now sizzling skillet for a good few minutes.

Perhaps the omen on the highway had caused him to be slightly unhinged, or maybe it was the thought of the new moon that was due this night. Perhaps...he was hearing things. Never had his ears led him astray before; but whatever it was that might be out there in the dead of the woods was keeping ungodly still. If it be predator, it was more skilled at the hunt than he.

He fetched his bow and two arrows, placing them next to his sitting log, and for good measure, drew his hunting knife from its stiff, waxed leather case, sticking it in the log beside him for easy retrieval.

Taking the wooden bowl he had cut up the fowl's meat in, he shakily tossed the slices of pheasant into the angry skillet. Wiping his sweaty palms along his cloak, he grabbed a pinch of white spice, salt, peppercorn, and saffron from a small container, dashing the greased meats with a moderate layer of seasoning. The searing meat thirstily soaked up the spices.

The night was quiet once more, all but for his cooking meal, and though he had planned to cook up some cumin and star anise-seasoned black rice, fluffed with the pheasant ghee drippings as a side dish, his appetite had lessened under the current aura that had befallen his cursed camp; and, though he did not wish to admit it, even in his head, he preferred to move as little as possible, as every fold of cloth or brush of leather upon his movement was causing his ears to itch with nervous acuteness.

He instead just sat there, idly watching the meat, keeping it from burning, his gaze being often drawn to the pheasant carcass across the fire from him, steam no longer leaving its open insides.

"Turned clean inside out," Gerun mumbled, returning once again to the mental scene upon which his day had revolved around.

A pop from the meat brought him back to the task at hand, the sight of the shimmering golden, reddish-browned chicken bolstering his mood, and courage, a bit.

"'Twas but a queer bird's call. How many years

have I been alone in these woods? How many nights alone have I survived under a canopy of leaves and stars?" Gerun's voiced reassurances both emboldened him and caused a slight tremble in his limbs all at once. He again raked at the flaking skin along his neck, attempting to soothe the mounting prickling sensation.

He lifted some of the meat to his mouth, sloppily chewing as he finished his proclamations. "Countless, I say."

In truth, he had only trapped the east side of the highway in this region. The game always seemed to be more plentiful there. Rarely did he hunt or camp on the west side of the road. In all the years he had gamed this area, this night might have been the deepest he had been into the thick of the west side of the Nightshade Forest.

"What—" a voice, not his own, boomed in a reverberating staccato tone somewhere to his side.

He dropped the skillet, his meal dropping to the ground, now clinging to the dirt and pine needles.

Yanking his knife free from the log, Gerun spun to his left, crouched, and could see nobody in his camp. He was scarcely able to see even a few feet now outside of the firelight's reach.

He knew he had heard a voice, *a human voice*, this

time. He leaped over his gear, rushing into the dark forest vale, desperate to put a face to his terror.

A tangle of roots and bushes caused him to trip, knocking his cheek along a pine's rough bark, sprawling him flat on the ground.

Some of the excitement knocked from him, he rose, rubbing the needles and shards of bark from the side of his face, tasting no longer the rich, sweetness of the fowl, but the sour sting of blood from his scrape and the acrid taste of adrenalin in his saliva.

Gerun gritted his teeth, sneering in the gloom, cursing his eyes that were attempting to focus in the night's darkness. Holding his knife point out, leading his frantic scan of the foliage around him, he stilled, trying to at least hear signs of the intruder.

For long moments, even as his eyes began to adjust to the dark that he was enveloped in, it seemed once again that the signs pointed to him being alone in the woods.

"Nothin'," he breathed, a whole tangle of emotions confusing his thoughts now. He yanked at his collar, forcefully stretching his stiff neck back to either side, feeling like it was about to lock up.

Slowly, he began back to the fireside. He made it no further than a step before stopping cold in his tracks.

Underfoot was a soft and twiggy pile that

squelched and cracked as his foot came down upon it. He knew he had stepped onto a small animal of some sort. But the slipperiness of it rushed the blood from his veins, taking the breath right from him.

He hesitated for a moment, listening, only hearing the leaking of fluids and feeling the wetness through his boots, until dropping his gaze to the ground.

His mouth was agape as he looked down at the same pheasant carcass he had stripped earlier now under his foot.

He squinted his eyes as he entered the camp, grabbing his pack, stuffing it with his things, the grease and dirt that clung to the skillet, sullying all of his possessions.

Putting his knife back in its case and snatching up his bow and arrows, he turned to hustle away from the place, back to the highway, back to sanity, but in an instant, the fire went out, once more leaving his eyes desperately narrowed as he tried to adjust to the sudden lack of light.

The coals were cold.

Through blurry vision, Gerun could see a small figure out amongst the trees. He ran towards it, yelling threats at the stranger as he closed the gap —but the gap never fully closed. He rushed through bush after bramble, the figure not moving, its back towards him but remaining the same distance away from him always.

"What devilry is this?" Gerun screamed, his voice raked with exhaustion and coated in mock anger. "You use me in a ritual, like I'm some lamb on an altar!"

He raised his bow and nocked one of the two arrows, pulling it back, the device rattling in his jarred state.

The small figure turned to face him now, and Gerun hesitated, lowering the bow slightly.

It was a young boy, face emotionless, soft, harmless. A face that seemed familiar. As though he had seen it earlier that day. But he had seen no other living person for a few days now, so how could that be the case?

The more the deadpanned-faced child stared at him, the more he felt he'd seen him recently, as though a repressed memory was quickly surfacing—the impending revelation frightening him to wit's end.

He could hear whisperings in his ear. He wasn't sure when they had started, but they sloshed their guttural musings around in his eardrums now, itching, raking his mind as a unified choir of the damned.

The boy stared indifferently at him. The cause of it all, Gerun thought—hoped—as he raised his arrow and loosed it at the boy.

Suddenly, he was the thing on the road. The dead man, looking up to see himself standing above him, looking down in concerned disgust. Mouthing the words over and over again, "Turned clean inside out. Turned clean inside out." He had somehow become the tumble and sprawl of all the raw innards of the carcass on the road, exposed to the air, stabbing with tender pain, wanting to be covered by that stretch of skin that once was protectively, warmly, over him.

Then, the next moment...he was back in the woods on his log, a pink, starlit sky overhead, knife stuck in the bark beside him, his pheasant meat searing in his red-hot skillet on a bed of unlit firewood—though, Gerun the trapper, he no longer was.

"Left my team roadside. Shouldn't 'ave done that," he calmly said, tugging curtly at the hems of his trim evening vest, turning to go back to the highway to prepare his coach for the ride back home.

"No," he said, all of a sudden feeling something was off. "This isn't right..."

His surroundings were muted, as though looking through a foggy pane of glass. Was he dreaming? He scratched annoyingly at his neck, blood starting to drip from his fingernails.

A face drifted halfway into his peripheral vision. He was trying to look towards it to get a better look at their face, but no matter how he turned, he could only see the blurry side glance of their features.

Chunks of earth began falling up. Some sections of wood dropped out around where he stood, leaving him in a perfectly silent torrent of bright colors with half a child's face in his vision.

It moved ever so slowly into full view.

The face he had seen...when? Just a moment ago, or a century ago when he had been Gerun, the trapper? Neither felt accurate. Time seemed the issue in his guesswork, as if the concept was utterly lacking in scope or measurement. The swirling void. The child, soft, unconcerned. Had he not shot him?

He landed, as if the land that had fallen away from him eons ago, now all decided to obey the laws of his once physical realm that he had been a specimen in, and snapped back in place, the location he existed in becoming the west reaches of the Nightshade Forest once more.

Gerun yelled into the dark of the woods, pain ripping his breath from him as his face and torso began splitting apart, warping bone, muscle, entrails, and brain matter into a flowering fatal growth.

Gerun was still. His limbs no longer strained with fright and awareness—his viscera exposed to the night's chill, steaming the surrounding area, his flayed face showing a red grin along his warped skull.

"Turned clean inside out," a child's voice overhead said in an emotionless, soft tone.

Part One: The Unsuspecting Journey

1
THE WORN STEPS HOME

The old mountain pass was covered in moss, the smooth stepping stones leading up the mountain trail worn down by centuries of use. Fog rolled lightly through the narrow passage, obscuring how much further they had to walk the narrow ledge as well as how far down the cliff dropped on the other side of them. Reza knew the drop to be far enough to be fatal if one slipped.

"Keep an eye out, and watch your step," Reza warned the five companions she walked the mountain pass with, though the warning was mostly for Terra, the youngest of the group, at the tail end of her teenage years.

"How much further?" Terra asked, and though she tried to keep the fear out of her voice, Reza could tell the girl was terrified as the fog began to let up, showing the hundred-yard drop to the mountain slopes below.

"Almost there, Terra. Just stay focused on the steps.

Nomad's behind you; he's got you if you slip," Reza said in a soothing voice, trying to calm the girl who had begun to lose control of her breathing.

They all breathed a little easier as the smooth stone steps widened and the ledge to their left stretched out, giving them more space along the path that led upwards to their destination just ahead cloaked in fog.

"This is where I grew up," Reza said as she took Terra's hand, the trail wide enough for the two to stand side-by-side now.

"I remember that part of the pass giving me butterflies when I was young," Reza said, attempting to ease Terra's nerves.

In truth, it hadn't. Even when she was a child, she had skipped and played along the cliffside without concern. She and Terra were quite different, their upbringings night and day, she supposed.

Terra had had a loving family; babied by her mother and grandmother. She had not known rough travel or the uncertainty of being a stranger alone in a foreign land. She had not been tested by the harsh world like Reza had early on.

Perhaps, even a year or two ago, Reza would have looked down upon Terra, thought she was pampered and useless, or not thought of her at all; but she had changed in recent years. Terra was soft and innocent, it was true, but there was a pureness to her soul that Reza was beginning to appreciate. It was an innocence that she had never been granted the chance to experience for herself. She supposed in a way, she enjoyed being exposed to that tenderness of youth, even if it had been off limits to her in her younger years. It was like a second chance for her.

"Reza? Butterflies? That's a good one," the large man at the back of the line grumbled out. "Tough it up, kid. You'll see far worse if you keep traveling with us," he added matter-of-factly as the group rejoined from single file.

Reza turned a baleful glare at the man, but the look was lost on him, everyone gazing up to the stone gate and mountain buildings beyond it, their destination suddenly appearing before them through the chill mountain mist.

"The High Cliffs Monastery," Reza announced, her tone bittersweet at all the mixed feelings she had for the place that she had spent many defiant years at during her upbringing as a saren knight.

"Reza...," a voice issued from a figure cloaked in the fog. "Fin, Yozo?"

"Alva," Reza responded as the sentry at the gated archway came forward, her smile widening as she rushed to the group.

"You came!" she exclaimed, hugging Reza tightly as she greeted her, squeezing tight enough to take her breath away.

"To be honest, we were not expecting you so soon. We had only just sent the messenger dove two weeks ago," she said, releasing Reza, moving to Fin and Yozo, clapping them on the back, garnering warm smiles from the two men and mumbled greetings.

"You sent for us? What for?" Reza questioned as Alva returned to her side, leading the group to the gate happily.

"You...didn't receive our message?" the saren sentry asked.

"Nope," Reza replied simply. "We made the journey as soon as Terra was fit for travel. She sustained a serious injury that requires healing beyond my capabilities. I'm hoping Revna can help complete the healing that I started."

"Terra, I'm sorry to hear that. What happened?" the sentry asked, walking them towards the large cathedral in the center of the cliffside town.

"She was shot in the heart with a crossbow bolt. I did what I could to perform a blessing, but...you know healing isn't my specialty," Reza replied as they stepped into the small garden courtyard area next to the cathedral.

"If it's a healing you came here for, then perhaps we can do better than Revna, no disrespect to her, of course." Alva smiled as she waited for the rest in the group to catch up before opening the doors to the chapel hall.

Reza considered the comment for a moment, slightly confused. "Very few are better at healing than her...," she said, thrown off by Alva's odd remark.

"There is reason we sent for you, Reza–more than just to catch up with you. Someone has returned to us—" Alva said, smiling at Reza's widening eyes, wondering if she dared to give way to hope. "—someone we all thought was lost to us."

"Wait here," Alva said, smiling, running to open the cathedral's double doors, leaving the group in bated silence as they waited for her return, trails of wispy fog drifting past them as they waited a minute before seeing two figures returning through the dark doorway.

"Lanereth...," Reza breathed, tears quickly welling up in her eyes, a knot burning in her throat as she started forward, the suspense driving her mad, seeing the features she knew and loved as the woman walked out from the veil of shadows.

She rushed to embrace her, openly weeping as she held tight the woman who had raised and cared for her.

Fin and Yozo both stepped up, their joy to see her alive unabashedly apparent.

"I thought you were gone," Reza sobbed, pulling away to double-check that her eyes and mind weren't playing a horrible trick on her, looking upon the graciously smiling high priestess.

She smiled, looking to Fin and Yozo, sharing a knowing glance between each other of the difficult times they had suffered together during the war, looking down to Reza to answer her.

"I *was* gone, Reza. Banished to the Plane of Ash." Lanereth's gaze lowered, horrid memories of the hellish dimension flashing through her thoughts as she spoke of the recent past.

She took a breath and mentally moved past the thought, her smile returning as she looked back up to the gathering of Reza's friends, most of whom she had gotten to know in some way over the last few years, adding, "Through the love of Sareth, and the help of Malagar, I was returned to this realm."

She looked upon Reza's face, running a hand lovingly through her platinum blond hair.

"What of Malagar? Is he still here with you?" Fin asked, Yozo seeming equally interested in the monk's whereabouts, eager to see and catch up with their old companion.

Lanereth's countenance fell, her smile quickly fading with Fin's inquiry.

"He...was here. Not but a week ago. He left for the north—"

The comment left them with many questions, but the way Lanereth was speaking of his departure caused them to hesitate on pressing for answers.

She could tell she was worrying them, and so she offered, "He was in good spirits last I saw him. Perhaps it would be best to discuss Malagar over supper. It's much too long a subject to discuss here in the chill of the mist. I'm assuming your company will be staying at the monastery for a while?" she asked, attempting to lighten the mood.

"Certainly, we would love supper," Terra spoke, slightly louder than she had meant to, quite done with the meals Cavok and Fin had been preparing for the group while on the road.

She shrunk, embarrassed as the group chuckled softly at her eagerness at the mention of food.

Reza nodded her approval of the comment. "Food would be great. Our trail rations have gone a bit stale the last few days."

"Alva, would you send word to the chef? Set a table

for ten. Make sure Jezebel and Revna are invited. You can take the rest of the evening off as well to join us," Lanereth said to the sentry, Alva nodding as she left to begin preparations and accommodations for their guests.

Reza squeezed Lanereth's hand one more time before letting her go. "It's good to be back," she sighed as she looked around the beautiful misty grove overshadowed by the old stone cathedral.

"My thoughts exactly," Lanereth quietly agreed.

"Few times do we open our dining hall to so many outsiders, but at this point, most of you are no longer outsiders," Lanereth announced as the wine was being poured, the high priestess making ready to propose a toast to the company.

"Winding have been our paths to deliver us here today. Thankful we *all* are to number among the living to be able to share moments like this with one another. In the company of friends—and family," Lanereth ended with a look to Reza, holding her earthen mug out for everyone to join in the toast, which they did, a clanking of glazed earthenware sounding as the table seating ten drank to the toast of thanksgiving.

The winds had picked up throughout the day, and

the chill mountain air was now biting as the night wore on. Within the halls of the monastery, however, the warm hearths and candlelight, and the bustle of warm bodies enthusiastically engaged in storytelling of tales and adventures since last the two groups were together, kept the supper hall warm enough.

"Reza," Lanereth quietly called after conversations between the two groups had bloomed, leaving the two alone at the end of the table sitting across from each other.

Reza put down her mug and smiled, giving her attention to the high priestess.

"Sareth has...shown me much of late. Concerning visions, fragmented...I'm not sure what to make of it all, but you have been in many of them."

Reza's smile faded, realizing the weight of Lanereth's confession, waiting for her to continue.

"I had sent for you for this reason, though from what Alva tells me, you never received that message. You had come for a healing?"

Reza nodded, answering, "Yes, Terra needs a saren more skilled than myself at healing. She sustained a grave injury in Brigganden. I did what I could, but I fear she's not fully recovered. She tires quickly these days. When she's excited, she grows cold, weak. Her breath leaves her," Reza whispered, keeping her voice down on the sensitive subject.

"I will do what I can," Lanereth readily agreed, adding in a warning tone, "though, the heart is a delicate structure. Take caution with your expectations. That I am a competent healer, it is true, but some wounds are beyond even a saren's talents."

Reza considered the foreboding warning for a moment, slowly nodding in understanding before asking curiously, "You said I've been in your dreams?"

"They're more than *dreams*, Reza. I know when Sareth is trying to speak to me, and over the last month, I've caught snatches of...strange things. I'm not sure how to explain it. It almost feels like Sareth isn't just showing me visions, but events taking place in present time; some taking place in the future. There are dark things festering in the land north of here, in the Crowned Kingdoms."

Reza took a sip of her wine, thinking over Lanereth's odd visions. She knew she was not one to make fanciful claims. Whatever Lanereth had seen these past nights in her dreams, she knew it affected her to her core, or she would not have mentioned it to her.

"Why tell me about this?" Reza asked simply.

Lanereth looked down the table upon Terra, seeing her happily ribbing Cavok in jest over some recollected tale they were all sharing. The high priestess's countenance was distant…forlorn.

"Lanereth, what's going on?" Reza asked, head tilted in concern for where her teacher was going with all this. "You wouldn't have brought this up unless…is this connected with us—with me?"

"I wish it wasn't," Lanereth whispered, drawing her attention dazedly back from the youthful girl to Reza. "But it is. You and that girl both have been in these visions. I don't know why or what Sareth is asking of us, but I feel…she means for you to answer her call."

"Terra—" Reza murmured, looking to the girl, "—had been mentioning similar dreams to me as we've been on the road here. I hadn't thought much of them. I guess she realized that since she stopped speaking of them the more I dismissed them."

Lanereth could see Reza's disappointment in herself. She took her hand and gave her an understanding pat.

"She was born in the Golden Crowns Kingdom, you know. It's her homeland. She never wants to return there. There are ill memories of that place."

Lanereth gave Reza a moment to reflect upon it all, staring down at the wonderful meal in front of her, suddenly not hungry, even though she had been starving just moments ago.

"That's no small journey, you know. It's a two-week-long hike to Canopy Glen along the kingdom's border alone. Not to mention the trail there runs through the Evergreen Sanctuary, Farenlome's domain. I know you're comfortable with her kind, but...her children...give me cause for a healthy amount of concern. I will not travel to the Crowned Kingdoms just on a hunch."

"This is no simple *hunch*, Reza," Lanereth whispered, her tone harsh enough to catch the attention of the others at the table.

For a moment, she felt as a child again, Lanereth scolding her endlessly for once again being too reckless or too stubborn. It was a tone she knew well from her matron. One that set her back instantly into her conflicted past with the woman.

Reza looked around, sinking back in her chair, aware that all were now listening in on their conversation.

"I'm sorry, Reza," she apologized, seeing clearly that she had been too heavy-handed with her rebuke. "I didn't mention much of Malagar's departure to you. His journey I think is connected to these premonitions I've been having of the northern kingdoms. It may be time for that discussion.

Lanereth looked down the table, seeing all leaning

forward, waiting for her to fill them in on what merited such a serious tone.

"There is a darkness, a corruption, in the Crowned Kingdoms," she announced, speaking to all now. "Sareth has not shown me directly what awaits up north, but I fear, if we do not act soon, the Crowned Kingdoms will soon be faced with a threat similar to what we just saw with the Southern Sands region."

All were hushed as Lanereth talked, no one prepared for the jarring shift in tone as she continued her dire story.

"Malagar...has a connection to the Seam. It's a dimension that none fully understand, and as such, is a very dangerous place. Only a handful in any given region even have the ability to access it, and fewer still live long if they continue to frequent its paths.

"I know little of the place, but Malagar...he is learning its ways. He began to become aware of a disturbance in the Seam currents a few weeks ago—around the same time of my visions from Sareth of trouble in the land northward."

She paused, breathing a tired sigh before continuing. "There is something up there, perhaps not fully realized by most in the region just yet, but the signs are strongly indicating that if not dealt with, terrible things will ensue.

"Malagar was of the mind that answering this call could not wait. Not just for the reason to stop calamity from happening, but...he itches to understand the Seam; and this was the lead he had been looking for ever since our return to the realm—ever since our long walk from the Planes of Ash to Una.

"One morning, he left without a farewell. Perhaps because he knew I'd forbid it. I fear that whatever awaits him up there is much too terrible for him to deal with on his own. I don't just worry for what is to come of the peoples of the Crowned Kingdoms...I worry for him."

Reza could tell how much Malagar meant to her. She had rarely seen Lanereth emotional, but she heard the tremble of concern in her voice for him.

"So, you're asking me to find Malagar, to make sure he's alright? I've never even met the man, Lanereth," Reza replied, hoping that wasn't what Lanereth was getting at. She had journeyed to the monastery for sanctuary and peace, the last two years of war greatly weighing on her—on them all. The last thing she wanted now was to be thrown right back into solving other people's problems, even if it was those she held dear.

"It's not just Malagar, Reza. I fear the trouble brewing up in the Crowned Kingdoms is of utmost import. Sareth demands us to—"

"No, Sareth demands you to solve whatever this trouble is, not me. If she wanted to call me to this task, why didn't she reveal these signs directly to me?"

Lanereth was taken aback by Reza's defensiveness, but her surprise was fleeting. She *had*, after all, been the closest thing to a mother the girl had ever known. She knew how mulish the strong-headed girl could get on the turn of a dime. She was never shy about making her mood known.

"Reza," Fin softly spoke, turning everyone's attention from the mounting tensions of the two women to the man adorned with knives along his belts. "Malagar isn't just dear to Lanereth—he's a good man with a sound head on his shoulders. And you know Lanereth; she's not one to worry over trifles. If she says he's in danger, I for one would not forsake him. He had been there for me, and I will be there for him," he entreated, hoping to calm the tone.

"I as well," Yozo followed up.

Reza looked to the rest of the table—Nomad, Terra, and Cavok—not sure how or if they should respond, the three not knowing Malagar either, and having no part in Lanereth's talk of visions and premonitions.

"So, what, you two would go alone into the north after Malagar? Have either of you even been to the Crowned Kingdoms? The region is vast, the kingdoms often contending one with another, and the trail there is not a simple ride along a highway," Reza said, more than a little put out with Fin and Yozo taking Lanereth's side on the matter.

"Yes, I am saying that. If Malagar needs us, then he needs us," Fin answered readily, adding in an attempt to de-escalate rising tensions between him and Reza. "Look, Mal is our friend," he said, putting a hand on Yozo's arm as he spoke, "but I wouldn't expect anyone else to accompany us to find him. Aside from Nomad, both Yozo and I have more time on the road than anyone at this table. We'll be fine, regardless of what the Crowned Kingdoms have in store for us. Stick to your original plan, by all means. Stay here for a season of rest and study. I'm sure we'll be back before the winter is through. After which, we'll all pack up and head back to the Southern Sands."

His casual tone annoyed Reza, perhaps even more than if he had been directly arguing with her. It was not a subject to be taken lightly. A dangerous mission, rife with unknowns, sprung on her over her first supper after a long journey on the open road was not how she wanted to start her stay at the secluded mountain monastery, and she was not going to pretend to any at the table that what Lanereth was asking of her—of them—was not a tall order.

"Terra, you alright?" Cavok asked in a quiet voice. Everyone heard the concerning question regardless, the man's deep voice giving his worry away as he rubbed a comforting hand along her shoulder.

Terra clutched at her chest, looking paler than usual. Seeing everyone looking to her, worry etched on their faces, she tried to shrug off their concerns.

"Perhaps today was a bit *too* exciting," she said, making an effort to smile through the debilitating episode, her heart struggling to deliver its life-giving resource to her body.

"I pushed myself too hard today," she added after wincing through chest pain, slipping back against Cavok's hand of support.

The room instantly became active, Cavok picking her up into his arms as she fainted, Lanereth ordering the large man to carry the girl and to follow her lead to the chapel's altar, ordering all but Reza and Revna to stay behind.

They rushed out of the dining hall, stepping out into the chill courtyard, their breath smokey in the moonlight, save for Terra, who barely drew breath at all, her skin color matching that of the pale moonlight.

"Has this happened before?" Lanereth asked Reza as Revna opened the church doors for them, the group entering the dark chapel, rushing down the aisle to the altar.

"She's had episodes of exhaustion, but I have not

seen her this bad," Reza breathed as Cavok gently laid her upon Sareth's altar, her breathing all but the faintest attempt at that point.

"Revna, Reza, join me in a healing circle," she ordered, asking the other two saren to help siphon lifeforce between all three of them to grant Lanereth ample time to properly perform her craft.

The two women readily placed hands upon her shoulder, and Lanereth gently placed a hand upon the cold girl's forehead and chest, initiating the ceremony of health, Lanereth instantly feeling a drain of life from her as she took in the process of death that was unfolding before her that she could now clearly see.

The young lady's heart had torn and was spilling red life from its protective chambers. There was no time to be delicate. She surged her focus there, mending what tissue she could within the ruptured vessel.

Reza and Revna trembled as Lanereth pressed them for aether, taking from them life to provide the girl on the altar a second chance.

The sarens knew the price of their gift. They knew each rite of health came with a cost, and they knew the sapping waves of essence flux would weaken them for days beyond. They knew well the price they paid was the price of life, theirs for hers.

Cavok watched helplessly in the dark as the winds blew through the open chapel doors, a chill entering the room as the three women trembled through the long labor ahead of them to save the girl. Even with all his might and strength, he had never felt so powerless.

2

DANCE OF CLOUDS

Cavok finished helping Reza unlace her boots, laying her in bed as the woman, barely able to stand, immediately fell into slumber in the spare bedroom in the monastery's sleeping chambers reserved for guests.

He had been with the saren long enough now to know the toll she took every time she performed a healing, and he knew with a bit of rest, she would recover from this one.

He left her in the peace of the dark room to slumber the rest of the night away.

The other two saren, Jezebel and Alva, had helped Revna and Lanereth to their quarters to recover, and Terra had been taken to the infirmary to be cared for by an elderly priestess throughout the night. All had been barred from visits until further notice. He had nothing left to do now but wait for Reza's recovery and word from the priestesses on Terra's condition.

It was still dark and cold outside, deep into the

night, but sleep had fled long ago from his mind. There was no chance at getting rest that night at this point. He would be forced to wander the grounds with heavy thoughts and worries over his friends' conditions.

"How is she?" came a voice from the shadows in the grove behind him. He knew Fin's voice better than anyone. The two had grown up together as orphans in the rotten streets of Rochata-Ung, after all. Fin was like a brother to him—probably more so than most actual siblings, he imagined.

"She's good—just sleeping it off," he responded, assuaging his concerns over Reza.

Cavok leaned on the low stone wall along the cliffside, looking out in reflection. Fin came to stand next to the hulk of a man, sharing the beautiful nocturnal view of the misty Jeenyre mountain range.

"Never have I been more lost, Fin," the man tiredly admitted, his voice slack, catching Fin off guard with the rare show of vulnerability.

"Oh, I don't know," Fin stammered, the comment catching him by surprise. "That one time you were eaten alive by that juvenile waste worm when we were kids, and we got you outta its belly, you were pretty lost then," the man chuckled, meriting a smirk from Cavok from the memory.

"You took in some of its bile and got all hallucinogenic on us. Thought we were the worms after that for the rest of the evening. Ahh, if we hadn'ta had good ol' Matt there to mix you an elixir..."

The mirth of the story died at the mention of their old mentor, Matt—his recent death still stinging the both of them keenly.

"A good man, that one," Fin whispered, sharing the beautiful view of the nighttime vista with his friend.

"Aye," Cavok simply agreed, the two enjoying the quiet company of each other as they reflected upon the legacy of the old pugilist.

"Fin," the large man said after a while, breaking the quiet of the night once more. Fin felt from the man's tone that his friend was reflecting upon some heavy subjects.

"I don't mean to go with you this time—to find Malagar," Cavok mumbled, looking down from the vastness before them.

Fin kept silent, taking some time to come to terms with the statement.

"It seems Terra...she's going to need to recover from all this...and I plan to stay by her side till she finds her feet again."

"Finally getting around to see the sights of the Crowned Kingdoms without you doesn't seem nearly half as fun, I've got to admit, mate," Fin replied after some time, attempting to drag himself from the melancholy thoughts of being separated from his best friend once more. Rare in life it was that they were apart, but unfortunately, the more it was becoming the norm in recent years.

"You'll have the foreigners," Cavok grumbled, his resentment of the two clear, which surprised Fin more than a little, his tone lightening as he added, "and Reza probably. She didn't seem keen on the mission, but I doubt she'd be able to rest here knowing you three are bumbling around in the wilderness without her. Plus, she wouldn't willingly leave Nomad's side unless forced to, and I saw the look in his eyes when talk of the Crowned Kingdoms started. He's a traveler—a nomad. Wanderlust is in his blood. It's doubtful he'll lounge at some secluded monastery for too long. This recovery mission is just the excuse for him to hit the trail again.

"And Yozo, he's bound to loyalty, like a newborn babe after his *change of heart*. If he has loyalty to this Malagar fella, he'll probably run himself into the ground to pursue and ensure his safety. It's likely all he's got right now right after his reformation, starting life over again. Usually doesn't stick, though—change that is. Old habits die hard. He tried to murder Nomad only months ago along the dunes, don't forget that. I saw the look in his eyes while he cut into the man's face. He was enjoying bleeding the life from him slowly..."

Fin had turned from the man during his rundown of everyone in their group, looking back out into the everchanging wispy clouds below them, barely covering the jagged spires of the sharp mountains. He supposed Cavok had mostly captured each of their companions' habits accurately.

"So what of this boy, Malagar? You say he was one of Matt's last trainees?"

Fin reflected upon the monk, Malagar. Matt had trained him in his own style of combat, the way of the fist. As a brawler, Matt had been unmatched, at least locally. Fin had seen Malagar in combat, and the similarities to Matt's stance and style were uncanny... albeit a little more sober as Matt often had a drunken swagger to his gait.

"Yeah, a real good kid. Still green in the ways of the world, but he has promise. You know Matt, he didn't take on no one unless they had a good deal of potential," Fin recollected, mumbling softly as thin trails of vapor issued from his warm breath into the chill night air.

"Well, best of luck to you out there. Watch your back. Take care of Reza," Cavok breathed after some thought on the man Fin had set to finding.

“Will do, mate. Don’t get too soft and cozy up here while I’m gone,” Fin replied, smiling back.

Cavok smirked, the two enjoying the night clouds playing out their slow dance with the mountain’s spires as the night wore on.

3

THE CALL OF THE TRAIL

"You didn't put your health at risk because of me during that healing, did you?" Terra timidly asked Reza, who was at her bedside in the cramped spare bedroom the sarens used as the infirmary at the monastery cloister. Rarely was it used as such.

Reza looked around the dingy space, thinking to bring some rags and at least wipe the windows clean, the panes clouded over with dust and grime. At least the bedding seemed fresh. The girl deserved better than this.

"No. If anything, Lanereth was the one placing herself at risk, but she's an expert healer. The only way she could be placed in danger during a healing is if she willingly sacrifices herself for the one she's caring for," Reza answered distractedly as she shuffled about the room, tidying up a few piles of clutter to help Terra feel a bit better about her surroundings.

"I'll have to thank her—last night was quite terrifying. I could feel the life slipping from me. It felt like Brigganden all over again...," she said, barely audible, a quiver of fear in her voice.

Reza had been right next to her in Brigganden when Terra had been shot in the chest, seeing the bolt slam into the girl firsthand. Surely there would be lasting memories with vast implications associated with that painful day for the girl for years to come. She hoped she was wrong about that, but she herself was a survivor of terrible traumas, and even with her toughness of spirit, sometimes, deep in the night, she would wake to past horrors coming to haunt her out of nowhere. Traumas she had thought long since forgotten.

"Reza," Terra interrupted, Reza not realizing that she had paused in reflection in the middle of a task. "Fin and Yozo just came to see me. It sounds like they are set in tracking this Malagar friend of theirs down in the Crowned Kingdoms. Will you be going with them?"

Reza came and sat down again, attempting to keep from being busy.

"I...hadn't thought much about that," she admitted, giving the subject some consideration.

"You should," Terra encouraged, reaching out to hold Reza's hand, smiling to the woman who had become almost like an older sister to her over the last few months.

"Friends are important. I know Malagar isn't your friend, but he is Fin, Yozo, and Lanereth's friend. You care about them like they probably care about him," she reasoned, contently peering out the cloudy windowpane into the misty morning outside.

Reza didn't have a response. Until that point, the situation had been a tangle of complicated and frustrating reasons why she should shut Lanereth's proposed mission down. Terra's childlike assessment of the predicament had cleared her head of rebuttals.

Heavy steps sounded down the hallway along creaky boards, Cavok giving a quick knock before entering the room, tousling Reza's hair as he squeezed past her. Grabbing a shabby chair, he pulled it up and planted himself next to the two. The chair creaked under his weight as he leaned on the chair back with crossed arms, resting his head as he eyed the two.

"You two having a secret meeting?" he playfully asked, getting a grin out of Terra and a frown out of Reza who was tucking her loose hairs back in place behind her ears.

"I was just telling Reza that she should go with Fin and Yozo to find their friend," Terra readily divulged, wrapping her arms around her legs under the covers as if she were devilishly giving away secrets behind Reza's back.

“Terra…,” Reza warned, giving the girl an eye that bespoke consequences if she continued to play around.

Though her tone deflated Terra somewhat, Cavok clapped a hearty hand on the saren’s back, startling her as he agreed. “Sounds like a great idea—god knows Fin could use someone to watch out for him. That one gets into more trouble than you could even imagine. Give him a new kingdom to explore, and he’d find his way into trouble faster than a hawk chasing a field mouse. Can’t help himself. It’s a sickness really,” he dramatically said, waving his hand in feigned exasperation. “Something’s wrong with that boy. I know—I’ve been around him since we were both tikes.”

Terra snickered at the man’s mock tone, speaking of Fin in a way only the two could about each other. They loved to play, she had seen on the trail, and even with their rough exteriors, there was a softness to them both when it came to those they loved. Those times, the ones where they would jest and jab, were the best times. It was the times when she knew they were at peace—and peace, since she had known them, had been so fleeting a commodity.

Reza on the other hand had not taken her keen eye off the man, her straight-lined lips not budging at all for his lighthearted tone.

"You think I'm joking, but I'm not. You really should go with them—take Nomad too," he added as Reza stared him down.

"The caregiver said Terra's going to need some time to recover from that episode last night, so she's bedbound for a while. Probably won't be fit for the road for a few weeks. I'll stay behind with her to keep her company in the meantime while you four set out for the Crowned Kingdoms to find Malagar," Cavok said, leaning back on the chair.

Terra jumped in to speak her pent-up feelings on the subject. "Fin and Yozo are going to hunt for him if you and Nomad go along regardless, that much was clear to me when I spoke with him just this morning. Would you honestly be content staying here idly by my side when your friends are out there braving the wilds?" Terra pressed, adding, "I know Nomad wouldn't—Fin and Yozo are his people. I know he loves you, but he would be ill at ease to stay here while Fin and Yozo are out there, perhaps in need of him."

Reza was getting ganged up upon, and she did not have good arguments to retort the two with.

"I'll be back to clean this room—it's a mess. You can't be staying in a place like this another night," was her reply, as she avoided the subject altogether.

"I'm going to go find Nomad," she added, patting

Terra's hand as she got up to leave, but a voice at the door stopped her in place.

"You won't need to look far," the man with an eastern accent said, running a hand through his crow-black hair as he entered the tight room, squeezing in suggestively close to Reza as he placed an arm comfortably around her hip. He was either ignoring the tension in her body or not noticing how wound up she was.

"Nomad. You'll be joining Fin and Yozo on the road to find Malagar, won't you?" Terra asked the man, having it out with the subject while Reza was cornered. She had seen the woman avoid difficult topics before, and she had to admit, she did enjoy watching the strong woman squirm. Perhaps it was a bit too wicked a habit, but she couldn't resist the opportunity.

Nomad thought on the question for a second before answering with a genuine, "If they need a third, I will be there for them. Honestly, I have not asked them of their plans."

"Perhaps it is time to rekindle last night's conversation then. Terra has been stabilized and seems to be doing much better. I'll stay with her through the morning just to be safe," Cavok said before Reza could protest.

"Reza, have you visited Lanereth yet?" Cavok asked.

"No, I haven't," she tersely replied, knowing full well Terra and Cavok were practically in cahoots against her at that point.

"You should. She means a lot to you," Nomad said, taking her hand. "I'll join you, at least for the stroll there," he kindly offered.

"I—" she started heatedly, composing herself before continuing, "will see myself there."

She walked out of the room, closing the door on the three.

Working through a few steadying breaths, she started down the hallway and out into the yard, heading to Lanereth's quarters.

The road had taken its toll on her patience with her companions, and she had been very aware of it that day, still struggling to slog through the morning, feeling like she was recovering from a horrible hangover from the healing she aided in the night before. She was exhausted, raw, and her friends were persistent with their proddings of joining Fin on the mission Lanereth had briefly laid out for them. She simply wanted a respite—even a short one would do—but to be called out back on the trail so soon after arriving at their destination...it did not set well with her.

She hastily stomped past the rickety gate that

housed most of the monastery's cloistered buildings surrounding the chapel, making her way along the pebbled trail that hugged the mountainside. She skipped up the gradual wooden steps embedded into the mossy slope next to the low waterfalls that rushed down the rocked cliffside. Lanereth resided in a pagoda-styled cabin that was tucked away, separate from the rest of the monastery along the cliff face.

The trail could get dangerously slippery in the winter, but luckily it was still early in the season for anything but frost to occasionally cover the mossy stone and dirt along the trail. She had walked those steps many times through the years, and as she marched up them now, she couldn't help but reflect upon her younger years. Things had changed so drastically between her and her matron, and yet they were still the same in so many ways.

They were both just as stubborn as the other all these years later, though now it felt like there was a bit of mutual respect growing between the two, making their time together, dare she admit it, somewhat enjoyable, where once it had been a constant war of personality.

She came to the hardwood doors, knocking loud and clear.

"Yes, come in." Reza could barely hear the voice from within.

Reza opened the heavy cherry door and stepped into the house that she knew so well—though something was different this time, she noticed as she walked through the living room to Lanereth's study. Her matron had always kept her living space pristine, everything in its orderly spot, but now, there were piles of books, clothes, odd items that Reza wasn't quite sure if they were household ornaments or relics of some measure of value strewn across the joined rooms all along the downstairs. It was out of the ordinary for Lanereth to live in such conditions. The image instantly increased her worry over the woman's state.

Lanereth lounged upon a long, low couch that faced her desk and large window overlooking the cliffside vista. It was a lovely view and it always transfixed her attention each time she beheld it. So it was with Lanereth now. She was not paying heed to Reza next to her but continued to look out unblinkingly over the sharp mountain spires before them.

"You're up and about—that is good to see," the older woman listlessly voiced, looking to Reza for the first time since she entered.

"I slept in a bit later than most mornings, but I've felt well enough today," Reza said, matching Lanereth's subdued tone, sitting on the couch arm.

Lanereth labored to sit up, Reza watching how the

effort tired the woman.

"That healing, even with you and Revna's aid, was draining on me, Reza," she admitted, looking her in the eyes now.

"The Planes of Ash...took years from me. Perhaps I'll never truly recover from my time within that hell. It has hastened me to feel past my age. There are scars I've taken from there, scars upon the mind, that have damaged me far greater than any physical harm my body could have sustained."

Her mentor had rambled, whispering as though her confessions were to a priest, shamefully awaiting an edict.

"That healing should not have drained me as much as it did," she continued, Reza not having answers for the one that had been such a guiding light for all in the monastery.

"A season of rest may heal more than you think," she finally managed, attempting to console the woman who looked more her actual age than ever before.

"Perhaps...but time moves on without care of us. Reza, I would head out after Malagar myself, but...you see how that healing sapped me. I cannot manage the open road in my current state, but I also can't allow Malagar to face the shadows I have seen in my visions to the north alone. I rarely ask of others from a place of weakness...but I'm begging you, Reza, please find him and watch over him, as he did for me while we were lost in the bowels of hell."

Reza rubbed her face with her hands, exhausted with the press from everyone to take up the task to venture northward. She had been in the Crowned Kingdoms one other time, and she had not enjoyed the place. She knew it to be a dangerously complicated junction of kingdoms, and depending on what side of whose borders you found yourself on, it could mean the difference between being set upon by hunting parties, jailed by lawmen, or welcomed as potential allies depending on the mood of the statesmen currently in office.

"I can send Revna and Jezebel with you—" Lanereth started, but Reza cut her off.

"No. The fewer the better," Reza said firmly, looking sternly upon the diminished high priestess.

"The larger the traveling party, the more answers we'll have to give to local authorities in each jurisdiction we enter. Politics are messy in the Crowned Kingdoms. Keeping things simple will best serve us if we intend to travel within the kingdom."

Lanereth looked in confusion for a moment before tentatively asking, "You intend to journey to find Malagar, then?" with childlike hope in her voice.

"Yes, I intend, Lanereth," Reza huffed out as she came to sit next to the woman she hated seeing in such a state. Reza held her hand.

"I do not wish to, but...if he means this much to you, I suppose I can't refuse to lend myself to the cause. Besides, Fin and Yozo are quite set on going, apparently. With their company, along with Nomad, we shouldn't have too much trouble finding Malagar and investigating this 'shadow' you say Sareth has been alluding to. If she will guide us, I will make my best attempt to do what I can in fulfilling her demands."

Reza had barely finished voicing her thoughts before being smothered by Lanereth, enveloping her in a hug, her sleeping robes drowning them both.

"Oh, Reza, you've no idea how much of a burden you've taken from my shoulders in saying that," the older woman choked through, attempting to hold back tears.

"I have thought often upon you these last few years. It's clear you've bloomed into a capable, strong woman. I know I don't say it enough, but I wanted you to know, there's a reason I'm so set on you taking on this mission and no one else. You are stronger and wiser than you know. I see your potential clearly now, dear Reza. I'm so proud of you."

Reza took in a deep breath, feeling very uncomfortable about the kind words. She had never taken praise well. She suffered through it though, and returned Lanereth's hug, the two embracing for some time in the quiet of the cabin, the first snow flurry falling upon the mountain range as they sat within the cold, dark house.

It seemed that she was headed to the Crowned Kingdoms after all.

4

A DECISION TO MAKE

"You ever think you could settle down in a place like this?" Fin casually asked Reza and Nomad, the three of them sitting along the lazy brook, watching the water wheel scoop up water, dumping it out on the other side in an endless cycle. Behind them was a quiet forest. Ahead of them on their spot on the bank was a picturesque cottage farmhouse and rolling hills speckled with patches of woods rolling on forever. The fluffy white clouds in the distance were the only things in the backdrop.

In unison, both gave the opposite answer—Reza "no," with Nomad saying "yes."

Fin smiled devilishly, knowing the inevitable squabble he had just launched the couple into.

Reza spoke first, as Fin knew she would. "I wouldn't mind it for a time, but to *settle down*, live a stagnant life among simple folk till I die is not the reason I put so many hard years in during my youth to train to become an accomplished saren knight. To squander that upbringing, I'd disappoint my people."

Nomad, ever the pensive one, responded after a moment of consideration on the subject to help explain his answer to the two. "Perhaps it would not be possible for ones such as us to actually remain rooted to such a serene location, though I think I would try this sort of life someday, even if it comes to an end before I do. Peace is what we all seek, and it's hard to argue that what's here wouldn't put most anyone's mind at ease."

Fin plucked a long grass stalk from the soft grass bed they were resting on, chewing on the tip as they thought on Nomad's words, the clouds overhead shading them a few moments before passing on their way.

It had been a little over two weeks since they had set out from the monastery, and they had finally made it to the fork in the road on the path to two different kingdoms.

They had discussed it at length, where they were going to begin looking for Malagar. They didn't have much in the way of leads, and they had met no one on the trail that had noticed the foreigner. From Reza's perspective, they could go west to the Rediron Crowns kingdom, or north to the capital, Alumin.

Both locations were their only real starting points for a few reasons. The Rediron Crowns kingdom was the closest to them, so starting there made sense, but there had been strange warnings from residents in Green Cove and Canopy Glen. Rumors of a troublesome string of murders in the land, and from what it seemed, it was not the work of a mass murderer, but some sort of region-wide mania known as the *Rediron warp*. The hearsay was worrying to say the least, but the odd circumstances of the situation, they suspected, could be what had piqued Malagar's interest. By the strange reports, it sounded plausible that the Seam could be involved.

Though, Alumin had also held great potential for them to uncover the foreboding signs and premonitions that both Terra and Lanereth had received over the last month. They were each closely connected with their god, and strong in their faith, and Reza didn't doubt that the gods were attempting to communicate something to them, and Alumin held capital temples of both religions, as well as a slew of others. If there was some *sickness in the land* as Lanereth had professed, perhaps the leaders of the great faiths could guide them to what disturbed Lanereth and Terra so greatly. Perhaps that spiritual disturbance was connected to Malagar's disappearance. They could not tell for sure.

Either way, they had very little to go off of and a very large track of land before them to search. Though they had delayed on the decision up until Canopy Glen, hoping to come across some clue to point them in the right direction, the best option either of them could think of was to split up, two heading into the Rediron kingdom, and the other two up to Alumin to seek religious consultation.

"Again," Yozo ordered, coaxing the young farmhand to strike at him with his two training sticks.

Fin, Nomad, and Reza watched the two as the sun slowly traveled down the sky towards the horizon. They had met an old farmer in town and seeing that they had a swordsman in the group, he had offered free board for a few nights if they trained his boy while they were there. They still offered some coin for payment, but Yozo did not slack on his promise to make his son at least somewhat competent at handling a weapon. They had been at it all day.

"Strike!" Yozo ordered, blocking the boy's swing lightning fast. "Other side, same thing! Good," he barked, walking him through the steps they had been drilling for the past half hour.

He held up his sticks again to go through the routine once more. "From here. Backhand, other side. See? One, two, three, inside, outside, backhand, backhand, and switch. Strike!"

Fin and Nomad clapped as the boy successfully navigated Yozo's pattern. He was doing well, the seasoned fighters thought, and Yozo's natural teaching presence somewhat surprised Fin, who hadn't known him as long as Nomad had. It was a side to the man Fin had never seen before.

The cheers distracted the boy for a gleeful moment, and he smiled as he ventured a peek at his audience. Yozo jumped on the learning opportunity, snapping the boy's wrists in his moment of distraction, coming in close as he rolled over the boy, flipping him to the ground, disarmed, with Yozo standing over him, stick to neck.

Fin and Nomad chuckled, seeing the inevitable scene play out. They knew he was likely not to make that mistake twice; both having been on the receiving end of the same whooping the boy had just been given from many different masters over the years. Total battle readiness was a trait drilled into one over a lifetime, but at least the boy was getting a taste of what to look out for and practice here with Yozo while they stayed.

"Fin," Reza said, grabbing the two's attention away from the ongoing training session. "I think it's time to make a decision on where we're headed."

The comfortable smile faded from him as Fin looked to the stream once more, considering the subject they all had been mulling over the past week or so.

"Yeah, I suppose you're right," Fin said, taking a special dagger only he could see from a fold in his cloak. Reza and Nomad watched the man handle the invisible object, knowing full well what he played with, having been there when he had received the magic blade. "Though, I think the path is already determined. Alumin holds leaders from many faiths. If there is some evil disturbance in this land like Terra and Lanereth seemed convinced there is, neither me nor Yozo are equipped to handle anything like that. You're a saren knight. Holy crusades are your calling. You and Nomad should see what you can gather from Alumin, be it from your faith or others there. Besides, you're the only one that's been to that city before or would even have any claim whatsoever to an audience from most of the temple wardens. Doubt they'd let me or Yozo in to talk with any higher-up. I don't even know what I'd ask if they did."

Fin twirled the spellbound blade in his hand, continuing his thoughts. "As for me and Yozo, we're both trackers. We'd be much better suited for checking out the Rediron region for answers to Malagar's whereabouts. This Rediron warp business could be nothing, or it could be the reason he set off in the first place. If there's signs of his presence there, we'll track him down and find him."

Reza thought on Fin's proposition for a while, looking to Yozo as he drilled the boy on the same exercise over and over again, making slight adjustments with each run-through. She had to admit, though the man was supremely antisocial, he did make a good weapons instructor.

"There seems to be wisdom in that," she offered, trying to consider any alternatives to splitting the group up. They'd be too slow in covering the land if they didn't, she knew.

"How will we meet back up?" Nomad asked.

Fin looked to the moon Phosen's cycle. It was waning currently, marking the middle of the month. He considered the time they'd need to search the Rediron kingdom, and the time Reza might need for collecting information from the heads of church in Alumin. It was hard to even guess at a timeframe for either task, but a decision had to be made.

"Two months and we meet back here at Canopy Glen, here if James will have us again. If not, then at the Leaning Oak Inn in town. Think that gives us enough time to wrap up whatever mess we get ourselves into out there in the kingdoms?" Fin asked with a smile.

"Sounds like a decent amount of time," Reza agreed, looking to Nomad for his thoughts on the verdict. He simply nodded in response, everything sounding fine with him.

"Something about all this...," Reza said, trailing off as she sat back on the bank of the stream. "My gut is telling me I'm going to regret jumping into this mess. Our objective isn't clean. Find Malagar, sure, but he could be anywhere in the four kingdoms, or maybe not even in the region. We're just going off of Lanereth's hunch. And the visions Terra and Lanereth had of some dark work going on here...the same could be said about any region. There's always foul deeds and corruption in governments and the large cities. The worst of humanity, those that crave power, admiration, and wealth above all else, work harder at it for longer, and they usually end up somewhere near the top of those societal structures. What's different about the Crowned Kingdoms than anywhere else? I don't even know what we're supposed to be searching for, or where to start."

The three of them sat in silence, thinking over Reza's words as the cool, gentle breeze ran a shiver through them.

"What are we doing here, Fin?" Reza asked, laying down in the grass, looking into the sky, tracking the clouds that floated by.

"I know what I'm doing here," Fin said, spitting out the blade of grass he had been chewing on. "I'm finding Mal. Yozo and I are good manhunters, so chances are pretty good we'll be able to find him before too long. I'd like to put Lanereth's mind at ease on the subject. As for you and hunting down whatever evil Lanereth and Terra keep seeing in vision—well, that one is a tough one; but sometimes we need to trust friends. You know both those women. They don't make stuff up. They're sure there's something here you need to do—something big. Your gut might be right. You might be stumbling into something dangerous; but it still might be worth doing and we'll all be there for you to back you up through it. As soon as we find Mal, we'll join you in Alumin. And if not, we'll see each other in two months back here."

Reza looked over to the two men at her side. Each had proven their friendship and reliance many times over. She knew friendship as deep as theirs was a rarity. Perhaps those deep connections had been forged directly because of the severity of trials they had endured together. After all, one can't pass tests they haven't taken, and they had taken many tests together, and somehow made it out the other side together.

"As long as I have both of your support, I think we'll get through whatever's ahead," she softly said.

"As long as we're alive, you'll never be without it," Nomad answered, taking her in his arms, kissing her on the head.

"Well said," Fin said, smiling. "Though I'll spare you the smooch."

"You take to the sword well," Yozo said to the farmhand. This time, the boy did not smile, still in a battle-ready stance.

"Good. We're done for the day," Yozo said, allowing the kid to finally let down his guard. The boy ran off to tell his father of the lessons that day, and Yozo came over to the lazy group by the stream, waving to the bunch as he skipped over the running water to join them on the sunny bank.

"It's good to know that at least one of us can make rent," Fin chuckled as a sweaty Yozo flopped down beside him.

"We should have just paid the man for board here," Reza said, feeling guilty that Yozo had worked so hard for their stay while they lazed in the sun most of the day.

"No, no," Yozo said, sighing happily. "I enjoy teaching. It's one of the few things I get satisfaction from."

"You are good at it, I'll give you that. Much more patient with that boy than I would have been. If you ever settle down, you should open a sword school. You'd do well for yourself," Fin suggested, closing his eyes as he laid back and began chewing on another long strand of grass.

"Perhaps I will," Yozo said.

The group let the afternoon slip by for some time before farmer James came to call them in for dinner. Few nights had been so peaceful for any in the group.

5

ALONG THE QUIET PATHS

The first golden rays of sun that day shimmered through the late autumn leaves as the four travelers stood at the crossroads. Nomad and Reza stood side by side, as did Fin and Yozo, the teams being decided on the night before and the plan details finalized.

"Another parting. This group of ours just can't seem to stay together for very long," Fin chuckled as he gave both Reza and Nomad a firm handshake farewell.

"Sometimes, solace helps one to appreciate those they are apart from even more," Yozo said, offering a handshake to the other pair just as Fin had done.

"Let's just make sure we do see each other again," Reza ordered, adding, "Back here in two months. Don't be late, and make sure to stay safe out there."

Fin waved a dismissive hand. "No need to worry about us. We'll find Mal and find you up in Alumin before the month is through, mark my words."

“Consider them marked,” Nomad said, tossing a small bag to Fin.

Opening the sinch, he pulled out one of many small sage-colored wads of compacted powder.

“Yozo can tell you about it on the road. You have a good walk ahead of you,” Nomad said, answering Fin’s open curiosity of the stuff.

Yozo shared a knowing smirk. He turned to go after one last look at the pair, calling back, “Come on, Fin. Let’s find Mal.”

“Best of luck in Alumin!” Fin called and went to catch up with Yozo’s brisk pace.

Nomad and Reza watched them for a moment before turning to head down the leaf-covered trail leading eastward.

It was the last day of autumn, and the crisp air made that very clear for them that morning. In many respects, the morrow would mark the real start to their journey.

◆ ◆ ◆

The week-long journey from Canopy Glen to Alumin for Nomad and Reza had been uneventful, relaxing even. Some nights had been spent in the company of fellow travelers along the highway, sharing information about people and places each had been to or were headed to. Some nights they had been alone, setting up camp along the forest's edges or along the endless hills and flats, enjoying the chilly cloudless nights, watching the stars track across the sky. The desire to continue this way together along endless distant roads had tempted them more than once.

"Come, come," Nomad breathed. He waved Reza to hurry up the last ridge of hill line before the landscape opened up to miles and miles of open farmland and hamlets leading to the great capital, Alumin, its spires shining like ivory in the morning sun far in the distance.

Reza slapped Nomad's hand away, refusing to hurry up to the ridge, knowing the scene beyond wasn't planning on moving anytime soon and that a few seconds delay wasn't going to be worth the extra exertion.

When she finally did make it to the ridge top at Nomad's side, however, her eyes widened as she looked over the vast scene ahead of them. Great lakes and rivers braided through floodplains, weaving around villages that were new since last Reza had visited. The great lone mountain West Perch loomed uncontested with its height across the valley to the left, and Alumin's broad walls stretched out for miles around the massive city monuments, a testament to the architectural geniuses who had continued to innovate and improve the capital's architectonics for countless generations.

"The population must have doubled since last I was here in my youth!" Reza breathed as the humid river breeze gusted about them, chilling the two through.

"There. That's West Perch," she said, pointing to the lone mountain. "We'll be visiting my order there."

"And Alumin?" Nomad asked, mesmerized by the sweeping cityscape still miles off from where they stood.

"Yes, we'll make a stop there first," she answered, trying to match up the image before them to her memory of the place.

"Shall we?" Nomad asked, extending his hand to guide her down the ridge, back to the trail that led to a bridge that crossed the river before them.

She swatted his hand away again, smiling puckishly, darting past him towards the bridge.

"Last one to the bridge has to carry the other for the next mile!" she yelled back, well ahead of Nomad by that point.

"You devil..." he murmured, bolting after her, knowing full well she was already too far ahead to catch, but playing along her sly game regardless, caravans and travelers roadside all but stopping to watch the two playfight as Nomad finally caught up to Reza at bridge side.

He grappled her, hefting her over his shoulders as he began crossing the bridge, the couple taking their first steps into the valley of Alumin.

Part Two: Rediron Country

6
CROW'S FLIGHT

The mossy evergreen mountainside stood looming over the castle Sauvignon like a foreboding, dark-green shroud. Heavy-gray clouds hung low above surrounding fiefs of rough-stoned barracks, homesteads, and acres of vineyards stretched out for miles in the valley below.

Sporadic drizzles from the perpetually gloomy clouds above caused the smooth-stone streets that led up to the castle to glisten.

A castle guard stood lazily at a corner post in the town's main intersection, occasionally peeking an eye from under his ill-fitted mail coif to survey the happenings of the quiet townsfolk.

He discreetly noted two road-worn travelers, hoods up, scanning the main street for establishment signs, watching them as they made their way for the Crow's Flight Tavern on the other side of the street from him.

The travelers' hoods came down, revealing foreign faces to the guard and the few townsfolk who were passing by, confirming their suspicions that the travelers weren't just from neighboring towns, but visitors from another region altogether.

The lead man was well-tanned—his face, smooth and handsome. His sharp features, hawk-like gaze, and leading position led the guard to guess that the tall man was the leader of the pair. His copper complexion marked him likely as a visitor from the Southern Sands region, the lands south of them. It was uncommon to have visitors from there, mostly due to the rough trails that connected the two lands, but not overly surprising. They did get sand-folk in town from time to time, after all.

The other man following the sandman was more curious to the guard. He belonged to a race of people that he had never seen, or even heard of. His skin was taut, a shade darker than his counterpart. His long, crow-black hair was fine and swept back. His eyes, sharp, taking in the scene.

The castle guard lowered his head ever so slightly, breaking eye contact with the group just as the man with the long hair looked him over.

He lazily looked down the road and grunted, leaning on his spear to belie his interest in the two.

A fogbank drifted through the drab street, and the castle guard took the opportunity to snatch a glimpse of the strangers slipping into the torchlit entrance of

Crow's Flight Tavern.

The sun hadn't shown itself all that day, with heavy storm clouds layering the valley off and on that whole week. Even though he couldn't see it, the guard knew it was just about sunset, the gray evening receding to the dark of a new night.

"How's your shift going, Sam?" came a whisper of a voice from behind the guard, just as soft footsteps sounded behind him.

"Marshal Reid?" the guard stuttered as he stood to attention.

"At ease, Sam," the quiet-voiced man said as he came into the lantern light, revealing that he was not dressed for duty, but rather in evening wear, a deep-green smock covered by a casual full-length gambeson coat. "Just checking on how main street's been faring this evening."

Sam attempted to ease back into his post, seeing that the marshal was not there on duty. He cleared his throat, eyes drifting back to the tavern across the street. "Na, Marshal. Quiet a day as any. No scuffs or nothin'. Just another gloomy day."

The marshal pulled out a long cigar and cutter, snipping the cap from the head. Taking out a box of long matches, he struck one and began to roll the flame over the end, gently drawing the embers to a perfect ring as he began his smoke, placing his things back in his coat pockets as he leaned back against the street pillar the guard had posted at for all that afternoon.

"Mind a bit of company, Sam?" the marshal said between draws. "Haven't gotten to spend much time with you since you joined the guard."

"Would love the company, sir," Sam said, the marshal's cigar smoke putting him at ease as he took in the rich musky cedar aromas.

"How's Captain Bar treating you?" the marshal asked casually.

Sam broke his gaze from the tavern's door to glance at the marshal before answering, "Oh. Good, good."

The marshal watched as Sam's attention drifted back to the tavern's threshold. He took a slow draw of his cigar before asking, "You've been eyeing Crow's Flight since I came upon you. Something on your mind, Sam?"

This time, Sam did look to the marshal in earnest, realizing he was splitting his attention before. "Saw a strange pair enter there not but a few moments before you arrived. Both foreigners, one I've no idea what lands he even hails from."

Reid eyed the tavern's torchlit façade while enjoying a few more moments with his cigar before placing a hand on Sam's shoulder. "Maybe I'll know where they're from. I've been a few more places than you, after all," the marshal said before ambling towards the tavern.

The Crow's Flight was dimly lit by a few amber-colored lanterns hanging from rafters overhead, and an open hearth at the end of the sitting room. The sounds of mugs being filled, the low mumble of surrounding tables, and the sporadic crackle and pop of the hearth tempted the marshal, the welcoming atmosphere promising to provide relaxation to his body and mind after the long day in and out of Castle Sauvignon. The last month had been hell; often he'd been on shift from sunrise till well after sunset. There had been so many preparations to see to—so much administration. A restful night at Crow's Flight with an ale and a cigar sounded like heaven....

"Brandy if you would, my dear," a tan man called to the waitress.

"Green tea for me, if you have it," a foreign man at the same table added.

Reid glanced at the two casually, confirming the two were the ones the guard had described.

He continued past them to the bar, taking a seat.

"Ah!" Ben started, noticing the marshal as he took a stool, but was cut short as Reid gave an eye and discreetly held up a warning hand to Ben.

Ben caught the marshal's drift, lowering his voice as he asked, "What'll ya have?"

"Whatever's on tap, Ben. Thanks," Reid replied softly.

"Sauvignon ale it is," Ben crooned, handling a beer mug under the spout as he pulled the tap lever, caramel-colored liquid readily flowing out of the spout, quickly filling the glass. Taking a flat wooden stick, he skimmed the excess foam off the top of the glass and handed the drink to the marshal.

"Those two strangers just showed up?" Reid asked, his voice barely above a whisper.

"Yup. Anne only just took their cloaks and sat them down," Ben answered, matching the marshal's volume.

"Mind if I order them some of your famous venison bacon-wrapped tenderloins? Just a side for the both of 'em, not a whole meal," Reid asked.

Ben nodded, catching Anne by the elbow as she passed, telling her the order that was just placed.

"Sure thing, love," she smiled, getting back to preparing the drinks that the table of three had just ordered, yelling the order to the cook in the back kitchen beyond the bar.

"If I wanted that order yelled, I would've done it...," Ben grumbled, rolling his eyes as he looked to the marshal, who gave an understanding smirk as he tended to his ale.

He had just finished his ale as Anne brought out the appetizer and a few plates for the table. She served the dish to the group and exchanged a few words, pointing to Reid across the room just as he turned to get up from the bar, waving to the group as he sauntered over to them.

"First time this trip we've been treated. Much appreciated. Care to join us? Pull up a chair," Fin said, a comfortable smile greeting Reid, contrasting the untrusting glare of the other man at the table.

"Would love to," Reid replied, pulling up a seat from an adjoining table.

He kicked back in the chair and blew smoke over the ash on his cigar, inspecting it for a moment before looking to both of them, replying in kind with a smile of his own to the well-tanned man.

"Enjoy," Reid said, nodding to the bacon venison. "In my opinion, that's the best dish Ben serves here."

Fin took a slice, forking a cut into his mouth. His eyes widened pleasantly. He smiled to his companion as he jabbed, "Wow. Months on the road almost had me forgetting what a real meal could taste like."

Yozo remained unmoving, clearly in no mood to be won over by the stranger's generosity.

"Try some. See for yourself," Reid persisted, looking to Yozo as he sat back, tending to his cigar's ash.

Yozo took a quick, calculating stare at the cigar man. Hesitantly, he served himself a slice of the venison.

Eyebrows perked up, and Yozo was silent as he finished the serving.

"How rude of us—we skipped right over introductions. My name's Fin. And this is my travel companion, Yozo. We're from the Southern Sands region. You must be a local here, no?"

Reid gently placed the almost spent cigar on the edge of the table's ashtray, considering his answer. He noticed that the leader had initiated introductions, giving only enough information to appease questions before jumping right to him.

Reid looked up, played with the tip of his mustache as he looked into the tanned man's eyes, and waited a moment before answering. "Yeah. Some would call me that—though that's not the only thing I'm called around here. Name's Reid."

Fin smiled back, an appreciation for the game of information they were mutually entering into with each other.

"You two been on the road maybe a month or two getting here? That's a long trail. Must be pleased to have made it to a major stop to resupply before heading on to—" Reid implied, fishing for their destination.

"Ah, thanks, dear," Fin said as Anne served the brandy and tea that had been ordered earlier. "A little late to consider an aperitif, but brandy is good no matter when you get it."

Reid kept eye contact, waiting to see if Fin planned to dodge the question.

Fin took a sip of his drink and raised a finger. "Ah, yes. Destination? Well, can't say that we have a specific one in mind. We wanted to see the Rediron Crowns countryside. Few make the trip up here from where we're from. We've got a bit of adventurer's blood in us, more than most I guess you could say. Wanted to see if we were missing out on anything."

Anne placed a hand on Reid's shoulder and softly asked, "You want anything, love?"

He broke eye contact with Fin and looked to her and said, "Another ale sounds good."

A moment later, Anne returned and handed him a full glass. Reid sipped the head off the ale before sitting back in his chair, returning to their interrupted conversation. "You do anything before leather-footing it? You're both well fashioned. Perhaps you have a sponsor?"

"Na," Fin scoffed. "No sponsors. Been saving up for this trip for some time. I'm an odd jobs man and Yozo's a tradesman."

"What trade?" Reid asked, looking to Yozo.

"Sword-craft," the quiet foreigner replied, clearly not interested in elaborating.

His tobacco-stained fingertips stroked the pointed patch of hair under his bottom lip as he considered a good entry point back into their conversation. Fin was effective at dead-ending lines of questions. Either he was just bad at casual conversations or good at avoiding subjects he didn't want to discuss in detail.

"Do you get many Southern Sands folk coming into town?" Fin idly asked, sipping his brandy.

"Not often. Occasionally, though. I might see a visitor from down south maybe once every other month?" Reid guessed.

"Any this last month?" Fin continued.

"None that I noticed," Reid said, the both of them leaving that point to tend to their drinks once more.

"So, Reid, perhaps you can help us. We've been

hearing talk of a string of murders in the region. Seeing the countryside is great and all, but since hearing the same rumors in both Canopy Glen *and* Tarrolaine, we're getting a bit worried. Have you heard anything about Rediron warp syndrome?"

"Ah. Rediron warp," Reid restated, lingering on the words. "Yeah, there sure is something going around up in Dunnmur. A few murders, I hear. Though, you make it sound like it's more contagious than what it really is."

"If it's not a sickness, then what is it?" Fin asked, genuinely curious.

"It's no disease—it's a mania. The Duke Lufairer has allegedly gone somewhat mad over the last year or so, after his wife died from a mysterious sickness. He believed the sickness to be witchcraft—some witch in the city placing a hex upon the duchess. Since her death, he's sent countless countrymen's wives to the stake…to burn," Reid said, pity for the situation clear in his countenance.

"So you're saying that the mania we've been hearing about, this Rediron warp, is due to this mad duke up in Dunnmur?" Fin probed, seeming to struggle to connect the dots.

Reid eyed the room, leaning in to whisper to Fin and Yozo, "Dunnmur ain't no backwater. It's a respectably large town. And the number of burnings aren't few. There's a lineup of witches burned daily, some say. The morale and mental state of the people there is broke—they're out for blood now."

"So..." Fin leaned back, gazing off into the fireplace. "...that's what this Rediron warp business is all about: witch trials."

"That's what it's all about," Reid restated, sharing Fin's gaze into the firepit.

"Not much to be done about that, I suppose." Fin sighed, downing the rest of his brandy.

Reid turned his eyes back to Fin, the other two still quietly watching them both.

"By two foreigners? No. I suppose not. I'd stay well away from that place if I were you," Reid murmured, taking another sip of his ale.

Fin played off the comment. "Looks like we know where to avoid at the least. Thanks, Reid—for the meal too."

"That weren't no meal—that's a snack. You want me to call Anne over? I'm sure you must be starving from being on the trail for so long," Reid suggested, about to wave Anne over.

Fin held up a hand, declining the offer. "It has been a long journey, and a nice bed sounds even more tempting than a feast, if I'm being honest."

"If you're being honest...," Reid echoed, smiling to Fin, who no longer returned one of his own.

The two left Reid at the table, Fin exchanging words with Ben to secure lodgings for the evening. Reid looked at the dark-amber draft—the ale tasted sweeter in this mug.

Anne came over to check on him after the two foreigners retired to their rooms. He fished for a few loose coins from his pocket, but Anne interjected.

"On the house, Marshal. We're just glad to have your company when we can get it," she said with a warm smile.

He hesitated, considering if he wanted to argue with the woman and settled with a compromise. "Just this once then, Anne. Next time, I'm paying."

She smiled, accepting the deal, touching him on the shoulder before bussing off to care for the other patrons.

He headed out of the warm establishment back into the streets. The night had come full on by that point, and a light rain glossed the smooth stone streets now, causing them to shimmer an angry golden from the torches and lanterns' reflections.

Sam remained at his post where he left him, his shift replacement there next to him.

He made his way across the street, the chill rain beginning to soak through his hair and clothes.

He entered the light of the street corner's lamp next to Sam, calling out to the guard, "Sam, your shift's ended. Go home."

"Needed to make sure you were alright with those outsiders. I can light your way and walk you home if you'd like, sir. Night's gotten darker than usual. Moon's hidden behind clouds," Sam offered.

The sincerity and loyalty Reid held with his men brought a slight smile to the marshal's lips, which he quickly dismissed, scolding Sam's doting. "You're acting like a damned watchmother, Sam. You don't think I could handle myself with two stray tramps, or the dark of the night for that matter?"

Sam quickly answered back. "You taught us to never underestimate the enemy, sir."

Reid considered the man's words, which were his own words. "You think them enemies? You didn't even meet them."

Sam's response was instant. "Treat everyone an enemy until proven otherwise. Again, your words, sir."

Reid looked off over the dimly lit town below, reflecting upon the encounter with the tall, tanned man and his companion. “Aye. There is wisdom in that.”

Sam waited for his superior to finish his pondery, clearly seeing that the marshal was in thought, and he suspected an order was soon at hand.

“Sam,” Reid finally said, completely soaked by that point.

“Yes, Marshal?” the man said, his posture subconsciously straightening up to attention.

“Return to the keep and inform the tracker, Dante White, that there are two foreigners at the Crow’s Flight Tavern that marshal Reid wishes to be tracked, both in town and if they leave town. Follow them to the edges of the kingdom, but not beyond. I expect to be immediately notified when they leave. After that report, you’re off shift. Do you understand? Go home and get some rest,” Reid said, returning Sam’s focused stare as he awaited confirmation from the guard.

“Yes, sir. Understood,” Sam answered.

“Dismissed,” Reid softly spoke, and watched as Sam silently saluted before double-timing off into the night to the castle, leaving the marshal and night guard there at the street corner alone.

The other guard was rigid at attention, Reid noticed. “As you were,” he muttered as he started down the dark street.

Dante was the best man-hunter in the kingdom —cold, calculating, relentless. He was overkill for a simple hunch, Reid knew, but it would give Dante something to do, if only to keep his edge sharp. And on top of that…it'd keep the man out of his sight for a good while. He didn't rightly trust the vicious man. He had been spending more and more time with King Maxim of late, and he had a bad feeling about their budding relationship.

They didn't often get outsiders, the Rediron Kingdom being the most secluded of the four domains in the Crowned Kingdoms. Not many trade routes or highways passed through them. He wondered what Fin and the quiet man were after. Something about Fin's answers didn't seem genuine, though the conversation was ended before any real answers could be gotten at, which nagged at Reid all the more. What did Fin have to hide?

Now, more than ever, the king had sound reason to distrust outsiders, and Reid had been tasked by the king himself to contain all rumors and news of the Rediron warp situation. Even if he didn't always see eye to eye with his liege, he was loyal. Reid knew his life was at stake if he failed to live up to his king's orders.

"Well, precautions have been made," he sighed, walking back to his quarters in the castle. He could rest easy that night, at least—and on top of that, with two pints of Sauvignon ale to warm his belly on the long walk back to his balcony suite in the castle's courtyard.

7

ALONG THE NIGHTSHADE TRAIL

"There's the fork leading to Fort Rediron," Fin said, pointing to the mossy cobblestone road that forked off to the left. The tavern keeper had said there'd be a section of cobblestone at the intersection. To the left—the fort; straight on would lead them to Dunnmur.

Yozo hung back, hood up, scanning the woods to their left. He had kept to himself most of the journey the last two days since they headed out from Castle Sauvignon.

"Alright, we keep straight then," Fin sighed, feeling as though he had been talking to himself for the past day or so.

"Quiet," Yozo scolded in a low voice, coming up behind him.

Fin turned, glaring at the quiet man trailing behind, but when he gripped tight his wrist to still him, Fin realized that something other than Fin's idle speech concerned the man.

Fin quickly caught on to what Yozo focused on. They could make out a rustling in the woods up ahead once they had both stilled. It sounded like gear being tossed about, as they heard the occasional clang of metal accompanied by scurrying feet.

Yozo had his hand casually over his sword hilt as the two men walked quietly up the road towards the ruckus, attempting to not appear threatening in the likely event the noise was just a traveler rushing to set up or take down their camp along the roadside.

Passing the turnoff to the fort, they saw at the end of the cobblestone section of road leading to Dunnmur a half-taken-down campsite, a man rushing to remove his hammock from between two trees, throwing it in a canvas next to his large trail pack.

"Good day, sir!" Fin called out from the trail's edge, hoping not to spook the lone man.

The man whipped around, his countenance one of fear and immediacy. He trembled out a question to the onlooking crew. "Y-you travelers?"

Yozo shared a concerned and questioning look with Fin before Fin called back, "Yes.... You seem like you were expecting someone else. Are you in need of help?"

The terrified man stammered out, "T-travelers

from Castle Sauvignon, yes? Not haunts from the Nightshades or Fort Rediron or anywhere the hell else?"

"Just...travelers coming from the castle, making our way to Dunnmur," Fin cautiously stated, not sure if he was telling the man what he wanted to hear or not. "You seem badly shaken by something. We're visitors to the Crowned Kingdoms; is there a danger along this way that we are unaware of?"

The crazed man looked about for a moment, peering into the deep forest all about him. There was nothing out there that Fin or Yozo could detect, but there was a foreboding silence along the forest's treeline, which caused everyone to carefully consider their surroundings.

"Did you see...a child on the road this day?" the man asked, hanging on Fin's response.

"No," Fin replied, asking in return, "Did you lose a child?"

"No, no, no, no, no," the man blurted out. "The child is not lost. The child isn't anyone's. It's a devil spawn. A killer."

"Is...does this have to do with the Rediron warp? We've heard many rumors about some madness disease up in these parts," Fin asked.

"The child was one of the first taken by the Rediron

warp. Killed many here along the trail." The man started, his composure breaking as he cried, "Gods! Rachel told me not to make the trip to the castle! I should have gone to Leniefoot or Canopy Glen and taken the lower price for my goods like she begged me to do! Now I've seen the boy ripper. He's here in these woods with eyes for me!"

"Hey, we're here. If it's back to Dunnmur you're heading, we'll travel with you. No need to panic," Fin said, attempting to console the man in a soothing voice. "We'll keep someone on watch throughout the night tonight in camp. You'll be well guarded, I promise you. We're no strangers to dangers of the trail."

The man was too distracted to hear Fin, turning to scan the deep forest as he scratched at his neck.

"Sir, we'll travel with you if you'd like!" Fin called again, seeing that they were losing the man's attention.

The man snapped back to eye Fin and Yozo, eyes wide and dilated. Without a word, he continued to hastily break down his camp.

"Something's not right," Yozo whispered to Fin. "We should not travel with that man,"

"We can't just leave him out here like that," Fin argued.

Yozo had no response, leaving the two of them to watch the man struggle with his camping gear helplessly for a few moments longer before Fin began to realize a disturbing fact about the man's behavior. Though he had been packing his things earlier, he was now wildly unpacking his gear.

"Sir!" Fin called out, more to stop the man from his crazy actions than grabbing his attention.

The man whipped around, looking at the group as though it were the first time he had noticed them along the road.

"You...travelers?" the man crazily called out, scratching at a pale spot on his neck, eyes darting back down the trail and off into the deep forest.

Fin and Yozo just stood there, waiting for the man to reinvest his attention to his endless packing/unpacking activity loop.

"I might be willing to agree with you after all," Fin muttered, backing away quietly from the edge of the road, starting them back on the path to Dunnmur. Neither of them dared to speak until they were a good ways down the road from the camper, sounds of the man's eternal struggle with his equipment dying off after a minute or two of brisk walking.

"What did we just see back there?" Fin asked, the first to break the silence. "And what of that man? I hate to think of leaving him there like that, but...," he trailed off, not sure how to finish the statement.

"But that man was not healthy. Something's inflicted him," Yozo finished for him. "It would be unwise for us to tarry with him longer than we did."

"Yes, but...he's too far from town to make it back to Dunnmur before dark. He's camping out here in these woods with us this night," Fin pointed out, initiating another halt to conversation as they both considered that implication.

"Perhaps it would be best to hike into the night, make it to Dunnmur before morning?" Yozo proposed, allowing a moment for Fin to think upon the proposition.

"Perhaps that's best," Fin agreed, adding, "The quicker to tell a guard in town about that man. Surely they'll send a highway patrolman to come and help handle the situation."

Yozo slowly nodded, agreeing with Fin's reasoning.

A storm cloud ahead flashed, thunder cracking through the sky, warning the travelers of the downpour that was soon to come.

No comment or complaint was voiced at the foreboding weather ahead, but a pall fell over them both—a sense of hesitation. Each played the encounter with the crazed trader over and over in their minds, questions with no answers sticking to them, like honey.

Lightning struck a tree ahead, splitting it in twain, catching both halves on fire just as a sheet of heavy rain doused it.

The deafening noise jolted each out of their thoughts, giving them only moments before the sheet of rain passed over them.

They each stopped and waited for the chill wetness to soak them through to the bone. They shivered miserably as another nearby bolt of lightning cracked off.

"If this be the gods trying to tell us a thing, I hope one of us learns to interpret their signs before too long," Yozo grumbled out just as the downpour rushed over them.

8

THROUGH THE STREETS OF DUNNMUR

"Gods, you look like you had one hell of a night!" the gate guard said as he came out from the side wicket door, getting a close-up look at the two travelers coming in from the Nightshade trail.

Neither of them had gotten sleep the night before, the constant downpour seeing to that. Fin and Yozo were no rookies to harsh traveling conditions, however, and short of being struck by lightning, there had been little that would have deterred them from trudging through to make it to Dunnmur as quickly as they could. The stranger they had met the evening before needed care and attention soon. If he had not died to exposure through that night, he surely would not last many more in the condition he was in.

"G'day," Fin said, his usual charm all but worn through due to exhaustion.

"Sure doesn't look it for you," the guard mumbled, waving the two over to the weather-worn table to the side of the road under an awning

They obeyed, waiting for the guard's further instructions.

"Never seen either of ya. Are you from out of kingdom?" the guard asked, eyeing the bunch from the other side of the table.

"Yes, from the Southern Sands," Yozo answered, seeing that Fin was not in the mood to play *leader* presently. Usually, he was the voice of the group, being the best at talking their way through situations. When he was in a foul mood, however, he could be more socially destructive than helpful. That was not how Yozo planned to begin their stay at Dunnmur, with Fin verbally trampling over a gate guard.

"Ah, sand folk. Haven't seen southerners for some time here," the guard chuffed, thumbs in his belt, sticking his chainmailed belly out. "Well, I'll need to take inventory of your armaments. You can have them in town; we just need a record of whatcha got."

The guard directed them over to a rickety table to the side of the wall under a tattered sun cover. The two began to fill the table with blades of all sizes; Yozo with his heirloom traditional curved sword set, both short and long blade, and Fin with a dozen or so throwing daggers and a trail knife, not bothering to take out his vanishing dagger, knowing the man likely wouldn't detect the magical weapon, even if patted down.

The guard looked at the spread of weapons, eyeing the two a moment, taking out a folded piece of paper and pencil before asking, "Your names?"

"Yozo," he volunteered, then pointed to his companion. "And that's Fin."

"Quite a collection here. Hope I don't see any of these again once you put them away. We don't censure openly carrying weapons in town, but you're going to stand out packing so much steel in addition to being foreigners. Might want to stash most of this in your room wherever it is you end up bunking in town to avoid any trouble," the guard said between jotting the list of weapons on a ragged scrap of paper, folding it up, and stuffing it in his pocket once he was satisfied.

"Yes, of course," Yozo agreed, speaking for the both of them.

"Alright, you're free to retrieve your things and enter through the door over there," the guard said, dismissing them.

"Sir. There's someone we passed on the trail yesterday. They...displayed some strange behavior. We were hoping to get this report to a highway patrolman or whoever handles that sort of thing here," Fin said, catching the guard as he was about to lead them into the city gates.

"Someone on the trail to Castle Sauvignon? Did you get their name?" the guard boorishly replied, not appreciating the extra work the group was asking of him.

"No," Fin answered. "We do have a description, though. Shall we give you the details, or is there someone else that takes these types of reports?"

"I can take it. Let's have it," the guard said, pulling back out his folded parchment, returning to the table to take additional notes.

Fin rattled through the situation report. "He was a tradesman, planning on heading to the castle town to sell some wares, not sure what in particular he was selling. Brown hair, tall. He has a wife or loved one named Rachel. Told him to head to Leniefoot—he didn't listen. They were worried about a child *ripper* known to be haunting the road to the castle."

"A tall tradesman. Rachel," the guard restated, thinking hard on the description. "Could be Jamous. He has a sweetheart named Rachel and he's an herb grower in town. Trades them to neighboring towns from time to time when business is dry here. I saw him out these gates just a few nights ago. So what was Jamous up to that worried you enough to lodge a report about him to me?"

"Something was off about him," Fin said, thinking

back on the encounter. "He was terrified of something or someone when we found him. Seemed disoriented. Kept packing and unpacking his gear. Aside from that...well, I guess his skin looked ashen in spots. He was scratching desperately at it."

The guard scratched at his chin stubble, considering the description. "Ashen skin, eh? See any blue veins along those white patches?"

"I didn't notice any," Fin answered.

"How about his eyes? Were they dilated?" the guard continued.

"They seemed so, yes. Though, he was a distance away," Fin offered.

"And neither of you touched him, right?" the guard asked.

Fin hesitated at the worrying question. "N-no. We stayed roadside when talking to him," he said after a moment.

The guard thought on the information, having no further questions for them. He moved to the wicket door, opening it for the group.

"You're free to enter," the guard announced, standing by the gate door.

"Don't you want to know how far down the trail

this Jamous is so you can send someone to pick him up?" Fin asked, strain in his voice noticeable to Yozo.

The guard looked at Fin directly and answered flatly. "If I had plans to send someone after him, yes, that is what I'd do."

"It's your duty to, is it not? That man was in need," Fin challenged, trying to keep his emotions in check.

The guard panned over the two ignorant foreigners. "If I were to go hunting after Jamous, it'd not be to bring him back home; it'd be to put him out of his misery. Sounds like he ain't showing blue yet, so maybe the warp hasn't taken him all the way, but all else points to him being on the path to madness. Believe me, it's better he's well out there away from others when that stuff runs its course."

"So, that was Rediron warp?" Yozo murmured.

"Well, by the sounds of it, yes, but only just the beginning of it," the guard grunted as another guard came trotting up from within the gates.

"Ivan, night's report ready yet? Need it for the briefing," the guard huffed, looking out of breath from a good jog.

The gate guard turned back to Fin and said impatiently, "I've got work to do. You lot coming, or going?"

Yozo guided Fin forward after seeing he wasn't going to be the first to make a move, forcing him through the gate. The gate guard shut the small door behind them after they passed, quietly conversing with the fellow guard as the two visitors made their way into the mossy streets of Dunnmur, getting lost within the web way of streets within minutes of entering its walls.

"The guard was in his right to refuse aid. If this disease is contagious, it was luck that we chose not to engage ourselves," Yozo said, counterpointing Fin's guilt in leaving the man, Jamous, out in the woods to fend for himself.

They had made their way deep into the large trade town, passing by many canal systems with the occasional ferryman rowing goods or passengers throughout the waterways and through the main streets they walked along.

"Plainstate soldiers wouldn't turn away those in need, even if they were sick," Fin accusingly snipped.

"They turned me away, multiple times...," Yozo murmured in response, remembering the hostile streets of the desert cities.

Yozo finished his thoughts on the subject, seeing that Fin was more upset about this than he should be. "You're feeling guilty we didn't help Jamous, I understand, but we still know little to nothing about this condition, and we need to be careful going into this, or..."

Yozo let his statement hang, too many people surrounding them as they made their way over a vine-covered bridge that exited into a market district.

"We should discuss this some other time. Right now we need to figure out where the hell we're going before we get lost in this damned town," Yozo grumbled, his sympathy for Fin's guilt-ridden bickering turning to frustration as the crowd's press began to force them onward or risk holding up the avenue's traffic.

"There," Yozo said, pointing to a food stand on their left that was nestled between storefronts and a few lush, light dogwood trees.

Whatever complaints and disagreements the two had between each other now dissolved at the sight and smell of platters of cooked goods.

They moved their way through the crowd to the stand, looking over the deep-dish platters over beds of ash, filled with all manners of meats, casseroles, fried items, dried fruits, and stuffed baked goods.

"One silver per plate and a drink," the dark-haired woman behind the stall announced to the three. She ladled some mulled wine into a clay mug for another customer, giving the two time to fish through their coin purses for a silver.

Each handed over the silver piece, one by one instructing the vendor what they'd like their plate filled with. The wafting aroma of the savory foods made it difficult for them to keep track of anything else. Even Yozo, usually ever vigilant with an eye sharp with distrust in crowded places, was wholly focused on his selection of delicatessens he was having the serving lady fill his plate with.

"We didn't stop for food yesterday, did we? Didn't even realize how hungry I was," Fin chirped, happily holding his plate of food and drink as he waited for Yozo to finish ordering his food.

Fin found a table for them to eat at in the market courtyard, and the two sat, beginning the meal even before their plate touched the table.

They sat in silence and devoured their meal within minutes. After, they watched the lush market square as they sipped on their drinks, watching the locals go about their morning business, reflecting on how they came to be in such a distant land.

"We'll need to find board for a night or two, at least," Fin said, finishing his drink while lazily looking over the market scene.

The two let their food settle for a while, watching

the bustling townsfolk pass them by. It was nice for once to be in a town big enough to get lost in the crowd, not standing out as foreigners, always being kept an eye on from the villagers or guards.

"From what we've gathered, it all points to Dunnmur," Fin said, still looking out over the market streets before turning back to Yozo. "We came here because we figured this Rediron warp stuff was in some way related to the Seam dimension. If it were, it makes sense Mal would have been intrigued, since the Seam is a heavy interest of his—more than an interest, more like an obsession. Lanereth made it seem as though that's why he left, and that this is where she suspected he went to. But if this warp condition is more a sickness and not supernatural in any way... then we're wasting time investigating it. It could simply be a pandemic, nothing more."

"That thought had crossed my mind as well," Yozo said, the two sitting in peace a moment longer, thinking over their next move in silence.

The crowd parted for someone, and they watched idly as those closest to the shady peddler across the street gasped and withdrew, giving his aimless wandering a wide berth.

The same white flaking ran across exposed skin, and now that they knew to look for it, they could see faint blue lines traveling across his neck, his eyes dilated greatly.

Before he could cause any more of a panic in the marketplace, the peddler turned off down a side passage and disappeared, the crowd re-forming and moving on about their business within moments of his departure.

"Seems the warp is well known to be within the town," Fin whispered, noting the reaction of the marketgoers before getting up to return their emptied plates back to the street vendor.

The woman snatched their plates and mugs as they handed them to her, busying herself with a new wave of customers coming in from the main street.

"Damn warpers," the serving lady grumbled. "They should go off and die somewhere outside of town instead of wandering around the streets, spreading it to others."

Fin and Yozo looked to the side street where the peddler had disappeared to, considering the woman's hostile thoughts on the inflicted.

"Witch trial tonight in town square. The duke is going to be there. Might be a show for some out-of-towners like yerselves," she spouted out, not even giving them time to respond, already taking orders from the new customers.

"I guess that solves our evening plans. Can't pass up a chance to see the duke we've heard so much about.

Guess we'll see if there's any merit to our friend's assessment of him back in Sauvignon," Fin said to Yozo as they started to navigate their way back into the flow of traffic, attempting to avoid being trampled by passing-by carts and horses.

"Agreed," Yozo sighed, frustration seething through. "Until then, let's find a place to stay and get out of the damned streets before these maniacs trample us."

Fin smiled, leading them off the main street onto a small canal dock. A small gondola was docked there and ready for passengers.

"Can you get us close to town square?" Fin asked the gondolier, jumping down off the highway ledge to the waterside dock.

"For the both of you, two silver strips. Quarter of an hour ride," the man said, rousing a bit from a daydream.

Fin whistled, whispering to Yozo, "Highway robbery."

"That congestion up there only gets worse this time of day headed into town," the gondolier offered, an easy smile coming to him as he took note of Yozo's tension at the comment.

Fin noticed it too, and knew any bartering play he was working towards was out of the plans now that the man had picked up on Yozo's weakness.

"Remind me to never play cards with you on my team," Fin mumbled at Yozo, handing over the two silver strips to the boat man as they boarded the narrow boat.

"Some apples in the bag there for ya," the man crooned as he pushed off from the dock, gliding them under the bridge closest to them. "And seeing how you two aren't from around here, feel free to ask me anything you'd like to know about our lovely town."

"It's that obvious we're not locals, eh?" Fin smiled, ducking slightly as they went under the highway overpass.

"No one gets as tan as you two living around these parts. Stand out like a sore thumb," the man said, making his way through his words slowly, fluidly, almost as though in tune with the slow drift of the canal.

"Is that why we're paying two strips of silver instead of your usual ferry price?" Fin playfully jabbed.

"Your need seemed worth two strips, am I wrong? I'm usually good at judging the worth of a need," the man answered back, no offense in his voice.

Fin looked to Yozo, who was still clammed up, though seeming a bit more at ease now that they were out of the crowd. Looking past Yozo, Fin watched as the backstreets of Dunnmur floated by. Though main street seemed in fair condition, most of the rest of the town was in shambles, a patchwork of rat-ridden hovels.

"No, you're right. Just giving you a hard time. Thanks for the apples, by the way," Fin said, settling into the cushioned boat seat, now determined to get the most out of his two-silver ride. "You know, we actually did need a guide to tell us a bit about this place. If you don't mind, I'll take you up on your offer."

"Shoot," the man offered.

Fin collected his thoughts, gathering the list of questions he had for the local. Perhaps two silvers for the boat ride wasn't a scalper's price after all.

9

THE PYRE

Fin awoke to a crimson light filtering in through the inn room's stained-glass window. The sun was low in the sky, and even without the tint of color from the glass panes, the sun itself glowed an angry sunset red as it drifted down to the horizon.

"Yozo," he croaked, sitting up on his still-made bed where he had crashed for their nap before the trial they intended to attend.

Yozo didn't stir at first, and Fin had to get up to nudge the man a bit for him to begin coming around.

They had been without sleep the previous night, and the full two days of continuous hiking had done a number on them, Fin could tell. Even though he knew they needed to get up and get out to the town square, he heavily considered just laying back down and sleeping the night through.

"Yozo, come on. The sun's about to set. We'd better get headed to the town square for this witch trial," Fin groaned out, rubbing his sagging face, giving himself a good slap to try and wake up.

Yozo did get up this time, though his eyes remained closed.

"Probably should leave our gear here. Wouldn't want to cause trouble like the gate guard mentioned," Fin said as he unstrapped and deposited dagger after dagger into his pack, out of sight, snapping his fingers at Yozo to do the same as the man slowly got up from off the bed, attempting to comply.

"I'm going to get us some coffee," Yozo grumbled, heading out the door, only needing to unstrap two swords, whereas Fin was still occupied slipping out knife after knife.

"Get one for me, too. Double strong," Fin called at the man already out the door.

The inn's main room, which had been filled to capacity when they had first showed up, now sat empty save for a few couples by the fireplace.

Yozo gathered two mugs of dark coffee from the innkeeper at the front counter, handing one over to Fin. They sipped the hot drink as they got directions to the town square from the patron.

"Careful out tonight. Those trials...they've been more like riots than public hearings lately. And with the warp going around like it is..." The innkeeper trailed off as she took the empty mugs back from them both.

Fin and Yozo muttered a thanks to her as they headed out, navigating their way through a few connecting streets as the coffee began to kick in, buzzing them wide awake just as they weaved in through the tight crowd that filled the public square.

The town square was an open yard, a few gardens, pillars, and statues here and there, spanning multiple blocks. All eyes were on the center stage of the yard at a lowered theater, where three large pyres stood erect, yet to be lit.

There were occasional pockets in the crowd, and getting close to one, Fin and Yozo saw why there were openings scattered about the sea of people. The warp was a very visual infliction, and the townsfolk knew to keep away from those exhibiting signs of the condition. The crowd shouted down and scolded the warp victims, telling them to leave as Fin and Yozo steered far around those pockets as much as possible.

Making their way to the large theater pit, they took a seat at the end of a row next to a tall limestone pillar. Hundreds, if not thousands had gathered there, and a communal hush fell upon the people as the blood-red sun finally set, the chill dusk air seeping in through the lively crowd.

A gap was being made by a group of heavily armored men, forcing the crowd back as the guards opened a channel for a group of chained women and some men to make their way to the center of the stage, followed by a few dignitaries.

Fin looked out over the crowd as the leaders on stage whispered things to one another, seeing to the last-minute preparations of the event. The people gathered seemed a mixed group. Some waited excitedly in anticipation, as though it were a theater performance they were about to see. Others were a face of disgust and anger, or of sorrow. There were jeers and stray comments of condemnation directed at the stage mixed with shouts to begin. It was a hectic scene, one that caused worry for Fin and visible anxiety for Yozo. They were dead center in the massive crowd. By that point, the masses had packed in so tight that they would not be able to exit the theater pit, even if they wanted to.

"Fin, look at the prisoners on stage," Yozo said, concentrating on the *witches* and the men accused of consorting with them that stood chained on stage.

Fin gave the lineup a hard look, attempting to block out the jeers and tumult of the crowd all around them. As the torchlight flickered and illuminated the group, he could tell there was something *off* with the group. The prisoners looked haggard, which Fin had initially assumed was the typical ravages that came from their imprisonment. But as he looked closer, he noticed the same ashen patches that they had seen on the man along the trail the previous day, except that most of their body had turned gray. A dark surface layer of veins could be seen networking across their skin. Their eyes were wild, each twitchy and filled with tension, like a deer ready to bound away at the slightest movement from a predator.

"Rediron warp," Fin breathed, Yozo nodding in agreement.

Another circle of guards moved through the crowd now, and everyone watched as a tall, well-dressed man walked onto the stage, flanked by two large bodyguards.

The man wore a striking blue vest, lined and laced with silver embroidery, a black wolf pelt coat, and a priceless sword and dagger set. His face was plain, black medium hair tightly parted to the side. The man was the picture of nobility...all but his skin, which Fin and Yozo stared in confusion at for some time. There was a sickly yellow sheen to it as it glistened in the torchlight.

"Is that...face paint?" Fin whispered to Yozo. Yozo didn't answer. The connotation of the duke covering up his skin color with makeup gave the two pause given the circumstances.

The crowd had died down as the man came on stage, all mesmerized by his presence, and the man did not wait long to capitalize on the calmed audience as he spoke in a strong, baritone voice.

"You know why these witches and consorts of witches are standing before you today," the man said, throwing his hand down, signaling for the guards to take the ones on trial to the pyres.

One of the shackled men wrenched free of the guard's grasp, lunging off stage and into the front row. A volley of crossbows loosed into the crowd where the man had fallen, ripping into the prisoner's back as well as hitting some in the crowd unfortunate enough to be next to the man.

"Retrieve him, lash him to the stakes," the man in blue attire casually ordered.

The crowd was alive once more, shouts of all dispositions coming through the din, struggling to be heard. Fin noticed a few calls around him crying out for the duke's assassination; others, calling for the witches to be burned.

"We shouldn't have come here," Yozo hissed to Fin, and Fin could see Yozo gripping tightly the space where his sword hilt usually rested.

The guards continued on with their task of lashing the crazed chained ones to the pyres as the man at center stage continued to speak, his voice demanding the crowd's attention once more. "Hard times we've had these last few months. I, as your duke, feel the pain of our people more so than anyone. Such sorrow has visited us—such darkness. So many wicked ones... burned—" Calls from the crowd of disapproval and threats of violence rose at the comment, but the man continued through the noise. "—Hard times we've had. Hard...taxes have been placed upon you. I sympathize with your plight—"

This time the crowd erupted, most all shouting their spite at the man, and Fin could see some in the crowd had taken up stones to throw, but the man boomed a command for all to silence. The crowd obeyed.

"I would make your burdens easier this night. A gift I have for you all. A gift of sustenance. A gift...from our gracious king," the duke said, snapping his fingers sharply as a line of covered carts rolled in through the opening the guards had made in the crowd.

Torches were put to the pyres, flame quickly traveling up the structures that the witches had been bound to. Screams from the prisoners cut through the clamor as the fire engulfed them.

Five large carts had been wheeled out amidst the ongoing execution, and the duke lifted a canvas from the center cart, showing its contents as the screams of the dying accented his gifts deliverance.

"A thanks, for your continued support through these dark times," the duke said, his voice cool and suggestive.

Pitchers of liquid, oats, rice, dried meats, butter, cheese, grains, and other dried and cured goods filled the cart to the brim. Along the sides of the carts each held large sacks of a fine, white powder that gleamed in the light of the fire. The crowd gazed spellbound by the cart's contents for a moment, the discord of burning men and women beginning to die out as they began to succumb to the torrent of flames enveloping them.

The duke continued. "I have pleaded your case to King Maxim and explained to him your difficulties… and he has listened. He has sent succor to Dunnmur. Sustenance to a weary people. Merciful is our king, and generous is your duke. None of this goes to my storehouses. All shall be distributed directly to you."

He walked off the stage, half the guards leaving with him. The other half separated the carts, uncovering the rest, and began to see to the distribution of the goods among the people in the light of the blazing three pillars. The scent of burnt flesh was heavy in the air.

Fin took one last look at the tribute carts before grabbing ahold of Yozo, yelling over the noise of the crowd, "Think we've seen enough."

Yozo broke his gaze from the charred bodies overlooking the squabbling crowd below. "This is why I don't like crowds," Yozo spat, yielding to Fin's tugging grip, the two of them shoving against the flow of bodies as they pushed their way out of the rushing throng.

10
THE WARD

A chamber pot's contents spilled down into the alleyway just as Fin skipped by, narrowly avoiding an unfortunate run-in. He was well used to city life, though. Perhaps more so than any of his close friends, including Reza, Nomad, and Yozo. Having grown up on the streets, he'd had the necessity of subtly keeping on guard at all times drilled into him from years and years of experience.

Yozo had opted to resupply that morning, while Fin had a lead he thought wise to check in on. There was no temple in town, though there was a healing house he had learned from the innkeeper, and according to the directions he had been given, he figured he'd be coming upon it soon.

It was not in the best part of town. In fact, the slumping buildings were the most rundown structures he had seen in the town thus far.

Asking a group chatting in the threshold of a shabby apartment for directions to the infirmary, they pointed him to a mishmash of what appeared to be converted old housing flats along the riverside.

Fin peeked around the side of the building and saw that the infirmary had river access. A boat sat at its little dock, canvas covering a heap of something he couldn't quite make out.

Looking around to the front, seeing no one along the perimeter of the building, he jumped the low wall along the side, strolling around back to get a better look at what filled the boat to cause it to ride so low in the water.

A draft of reeking putridity assaulted him as he moved towards the back of the yard, and he pulled a rag from his pocket to cover his mouth and nose as he crept towards the backyard.

He slid to the side of the building as someone slammed open the back door, chancing a glance as the person huffed their way down the streambank to the boat, dropping their payload on the dock as they threw back the canvas covering the contents of the boat.

A heap of bodies filled the hull, only a small space left open for whoever's unfortunate position it was to navigate the rank flesh cart downstream.

The man hefted the last body on top of the pile, adding to the stack of what must have been a dozen or so bodies, then covered the pile again with the canvas, fetching the boat's guiding pole and setting off down the lazy stream.

"Hey, what are you sneaking around back here for?" came a voice from the street. A plain-faced woman with auburn braided buns stood there, the scowl on her face telling Fin she was not going to be smooth-talked.

Fin came out from the side yard, heading up front to answer the woman, putting his rag away.

"I came to ask someone here a few questions. No one was out front, so I went around back," Fin said, hoping that leveling with the woman was going to soften her up enough to a cooperative level.

The woman eyed him, considering what to do with the suspicious man. She appeared to not be in a position to dally, Fin thought as her blue utilitarian dress was stained in fresh blood and gore. It was possible she had patients to attend to.

"I don't want to be a bother; I can leave if that helps. I did, however, travel across town to talk with a staff member here. If I could have a moment to ask a few questions—" Fin started, but the woman cut him off.

"—I don't have a few moments, but if you want, come into the lobby and maybe someone can talk with you on break."

The woman didn't wait to see if Fin was following her, hurrying back in through the front door. Fin was quick to catch up, rushing into the lobby, catching a glimpse of the woman scurrying off down a hallway into another wing of the building.

He did not follow her though, thinking it best to wait, as she had told him to do, for someone to show up in the lobby to speak with.

The room was mostly empty, save for a few crude wooden chairs along the entrance wall and a desk on the other side of the room. He peered down both hallways but found no sign of anyone in either direction.

Screams sounded down the way the woman had ran off to, followed by moans and sobs. Someone began muttering somewhere down the other hallway, not far from the room he was in. He looked down both hallways once more, wondering if any attendant was even stationed to the front desk. He slipped down the hallway the muttering was coming from.

He passed by an empty room, and another, and came to the closed door that the voice was coming from. Though the door was closed, there was a square opening covered by bars at eye level that allowed Fin a peek into the room.

There was a torn-up cot in the room and the plaster

along the wall had been shattered in pieces, exposing the wooden wallboards underneath. Chunks of paint and plaster speckled the floor. There were no windows in the room, and the only light that entered was from the dim hallway.

The mumbling stopped, and Fin stood on his tippytoes to see if he could get a better view of the whole room, attempting to view the person who had been chanting in it for the last minute or so.

He couldn't see anyone from where he stood. The only place the person could be hiding was on the ceiling, or just below the door slot, right up against the other side of the door.

A tense hand grabbed his shoulder, pulling him aside roughly, setting him on his heels.

Another woman, younger, dressed in the same heavy blue dress held him tightly by the wrist as she hissed out, "You shouldn't be back here, especially peeping around that door."

"Who's in that room? I thought this was supposed to be an infirmary, not an asylum," Fin said after regaining his composure from the woman's startling appearance.

She looked back at the dark room, concern clear on her features as the whispering from within the room started up again, barely audible.

She pulled Fin along back to the lobby room, saying in a low voice, "We had to lock that one away—their condition progressed too fast for us to evict them. Now we're going to have to wait for him to..." she trailed off, pulling her gaze from the dark hallway back to Fin. "...Why are you here?"

"I...had questions," Fin said distractedly. "Waiting for him to what?"

The young woman gave a firm glare. "I'm going to ask again: Who are you and why are you here?"

He could tell he was going to get nowhere with the woman on the unanswered subject, so he dropped it, thinking of the reason he had come to the healing house in the first place.

"My name's Fin. I had some questions I thought I might find answers to here. I want to know more about Rediron warp."

"You're not from around here, are you," she stated, more than asked. She looked Fin up and down, startling as another scream echoed down the hallway.

"Is that what all those people loaded on the boat out back died from? Is it a sickness, a mental condition? Everyone's giving me conflicting answers," Fin asked.

"It's a...well, no one knows what it is and what causes it, really. We know the symptoms, when cases began to show up, rates of increase, the duration of its course—but what exactly it is and how it transmits, no one I work with knows that at least," she said, opening up slightly to Fin on the subject.

"I think I saw someone in the woods with it, and a few cases in town, but mind telling me what to look for?" he asked.

"It's become much more widespread of late—there's cases all across town. Skin discoloration, itchiness, repetitive habits, vomiting, difficulty swallowing, stiff neck, seizures; with the really advanced cases, veins show blue through the ashen skin, dilated pupils, seizures, hallucinations...," she rambled, and Fin realized the list probably was longer, but she abbreviated it as she was not sure how much information Fin was fishing for.

"Hallucinations? How bad?" he asked, prompting her to continue her description.

"It's a funny thing; most times hallucinations are a symptom of a sickness. Any two patients will have their own fever dreams, but with this...they seem to be a shared psychosis. They all talk about a thing or being called *Umbraz*. It's hard to make sense of their babblings, but it's always similar," she said, attempting to explain the strange feature.

"*Umbraz...*," Fin whispered, hanging on the word for a moment before a thought came to him. "So how long does it take for a case to run its course?"

"It varies. Some, very quick—a day or two; others, a few weeks. Perhaps the condition's progress depends on their exposure levels?" she offered.

"Exposure to what?" Fin asked.

"No one knows, like I said earlier. There's only speculation at this point. No evidence has surfaced to indicate the likely source," she sighed.

"What's speculated?" Fin pressed.

"I don't know. You can go to any market and hear ten different theories about what's causing it. Doesn't make it any more likely than most of what's floating around out there about it," was the best she could offer, frustration of the lack of information she was able to give him evident in her expression.

"I've heard enough of street theories. I want to know what you think. If you had to guess, what would you say this is all coming from?" Fin said, trying to pull an educated guess from her. He figured that she was in a more reputable position than most to offer their thoughts on the subject.

"I'm just a nurse, Fin, I'm not the most senior attending member here," she said, slightly flattered by Fin's appraisal of her.

"But if you had to guess, even if it's just a baseless

hunch, what would you consider a good place to start searching for an answer to what this is?" he asked.

"Well...cases did start showing up here about a year ago. That's around the time," she started, trying to recall the events at that time. "I guess two things happened around that time. Sauvignon started trading some new spice that was a big deal for a while. Traders couldn't get enough of it. That was also right around the time sightings at Fort Rediron began to circulate. Aside from the duchess dying and the duke going on a witch hunt, can't say much else different was happening around that time. The duke has gotten progressively worse. He's not taking his wife's death well."

"Spice? You make it sound like supply has dried up. Can you still get it?" Fin asked.

She shrugged. "Apparently since last night, that'd be a yes. I hear the duke offloaded a ton into the hands of the townsfolk who were at the burning last night, along with a ton of staple foods."

Fin rubbed his chin, recalling the food carts the night earlier. "What's this spice look like? I'm interested in trying some."

"It's pure white. Looks like salt, but the granules are long, like broken needles. Hard to describe—sorry. I'm not sure what it tastes like—never got the chance to try it myself—but others I know said it's quite flavorful," she offered.

Fin waved her off the subject, not seeing that a flavoring had much to do with the warp. "What about the sightings at the fort? What kind of sightings are we talking about?"

She gladly changed subjects. "Fort Rediron is, or was, abandoned. It's been decommissioned for the better part of a century. As the size of Rediron's army dwindled, the fort wasn't needed. All troops these days are housed in the castle's countryside. A year ago, lights started to be spotted by the roadside camp between here and Leniefoot. Many investigated, and many swear there's strange folk living there, but the duke quickly put out town orders that no one is to trespass there. Something about the structure being too dangerous for the public. He went as far as to warn anyone found there will be tried as a witch. Said witches have been going there to practice their dark craft and hexes and banned all from the grounds."

"Wow. This duke sounds like a great guy," Fin dryly stated.

"He's not taken his wife's death well," she again said.

Murmurings began to start up once again in the room he had been peering in earlier, drawing both their gazes.

"Look, Fin. I need to go, and if you're not sick and there's no one here for you to visit, so do you," she said, her hard tone having softened considerably after talking with him over the last few minutes.

"One last thing before you go," he said, tugging on her sleeve.

She turned back to Fin, allowing him one more question before she went back to her duties.

"That person in that locked dark room. They have the warp, don't they?" he asked, sure that he already knew the answer.

She nodded a yes, brushing her hair back.

"What are you going to do to them?" he asked, the two holding each other's gaze.

"Nothing," she said, adding quietly, "Until it's their turn for a boat ride." She turned to go for good this time, hurrying off down the hallway, giving a wide berth to the locked door as she passed by.

11

WITHIN BLOODSTAINED WALLS

His head whirled for the hundredth time, a sense of falling dropping him to the ground. His face smashed into the grimy stone floor as a hooded man stood over him, waiting for him to settle.

Malagar tried to get up, but his damaged inner ear forbade him any sense of balance, causing him to writhe on the floor like a newborn babe attempting to acclimate to his new sense of self.

He held his head up, forcing himself to stabilize as his ears dripped gobs of blood on the floor beneath him. His victory in acquiring a position not in the dirt was short-lived as a heavy boot from the cloaked man slammed into the back of his neck, popping it loudly. For a moment, he wondered if the kick had broken his neck, but as he went to roll over on his back, both he and the robed man knew his spine was still intact.

"Surely you must wish for a reprieve from this treatment, Mister Malagar," the cloaked man sighed, tired of the hour-long beating he had given the man and receiving no new information from him.

He pulled the metal spike back out from beneath his robes, showing it to the bloodied man on the floor. “How did you come across that tooth?” the man calmly asked, pointing to the phosphorescent shard of bone on a bloody platter across the room on the table.

Malagar looked to the tooth that shined brightly in the dim chamber, then looked to the ragged gash in his arm where they’d extracted it from. His wounds were too deep. They weren’t going to treat the exposed flesh. He knew it was going to get infected and he would die a slow death within the dirt-covered white walls of that hellish place.

He spat at the man and missed, but the effort was enough to make the man forget about the tooth for a few minutes, focusing completely on the beating he gave Malagar that blacked the man out for the evening.

Filthy water sloshed in his face, forcing Malagar to get up to avoid drowning in the muck beneath him. Coughing and sputtering, a boot cracked into his face, breaking his nose and cracking his skull as his head bounced off the stone floor, a new flow of blood spurting from fresh gashes along both sides of his head.

"Wake up, filth," the hooded man spat, allowing Malagar a moment to stop the world from spinning. Unfortunately, since being impaled in the ear by the spike, it hadn't stopped spinning for even a moment, and now was no different.

"Here," the man said quietly, tossing a snow-white loaf of bread in front of Malagar. "Eat."

Malagar looked at the white loaf, now covered in muck that he wallowed in, its pureness tainted by his surroundings.

He looked up to the hooded man, his face obscured by the large folds of white cloth that hung over his head. "May you rot in whatever hell you worship," he calmly said.

The man sat there, eyes locked on his prisoner for a moment before a scream down the hall rang out, the shrill voice turning into a gurgle before slowly, oh so slowly, dying out into silence once again.

The man moved to grab the white loaf, picking it up and grabbing the back of Malagar's head. He violently smashed it into Malagar's face, shoving it so forcefully into his mouth that he felt teeth snap away from roots as the dry, chalky bread loaf was crammed down his throat. He swallowed out of desperation to breathe more than anything.

Sharp shards of teeth and crust scraped down his

gullet as he received an elbow to his broken nose and mouth, knocking out even more teeth.

The blows kept coming, and before he blacked out, he, for the first time since his stay there at that accursed place, lost all hope of ever making it out of that damnable room ever again.

12
EZEL

Yozo knocked a second time on the little shack's door at the edge of town. The guard who had welcomed them into town had been on shift again that morning, and thankfully, he was feeling generous enough to provide Yozo with directions to Jamous' house. He explained that he wished to update Jamous' significant other of her partner's whereabouts.

He could hear someone within the rickety shack, so he waited another few moments before raising his hand a third time to knock at the door. The door opened before he could.

A haggard woman, looking very sleep-deprived, stood at the door, looking at Yozo with a stare that he had seen before. It was the look of the hopeless—the look of one who had lost something irreplaceable.

"Miss, are you Rachel, Jamous' wife?"

"Aye," she said, her voice barely a whisper.

Yozo heard someone stirring within the small, one-room dwelling. He looked over her shoulder to see a small figure writhing in holey blankets on the room's one bed.

"He had the warp, didn't he?" she asked, her tone indicating that she already knew the answer.

"I…think so. I was the last to see him on the road two days ago," Yozo said, considering his words carefully. "Was Jamous showing signs before he left for the road?"

The small woman turned to look at the writhing mass on the bed and left to go uncover the drab blankets from the child's face to allow her to breathe better.

The girl's face was wincing in agony as she struggled to get comfortable, her colorless skin flaky and pallid.

The mother turned and looked to Yozo again after the child settled a bit. "I worried Jamous had it after Ezel began showing symptoms."

Yozo watched Ezel's pain-wracked face strain, her neck muscles locked up and tight as she struggled to swallow.

Yozo cleared his throat, looking back to the mother. "Jamous seemed affected by the warp, though he seemed unharmed other than that when I passed him on the road to Sauvignon. I am a foreigner. I don't know much about this sickness, so I did not approach him. I'm sorry I could not give you more information than this about your partner. I felt it important to give you that, at least."

"Mommy," Ezel's small voice gasped out. Both turned their attention to the struggling child. "There's voices...my head hurts!" she screamed as she scratched at her eyes.

Rachel clutched her daughter's small hands, weeping as she did so.

Yozo turned away, shutting his eyes tight as Ezel's frightened screams drilled into his soul.

He rarely retreated from his foes, but against the girl's torment, he could not bear to stay a moment longer. He left back to the inn to meet up with Fin, and from there, he was going to find whoever was responsible for the Rediron warp and kill them very, very slowly.

Yozo returned to the inn room late that evening, the trip across town and tracking Rachel down costing him most of the day. Fin had returned from his visit to the infirmary some time earlier, brooding in the lounge area downstairs, thinking over his conversation with the nurse while drawing down stacks of ragweed in his pipe.

The two met eyes upon Yozo's return, and both headed upstairs to their shared room, closing the door behind them.

"You find anything on the warp or on Mal?" Fin asked, whispering to Yozo, who was looking out their room's window overlooking the busy street below.

Even as Yozo thought on the question, he could see a stumbling maniac terrorizing the crowds of evening traffic below. No doubt, another victim of the warp. Yozo closed his eyes, the shrill screams of the young girl still echoing in his head.

"I…found something. On the warp at least. I don't know, perhaps this is exactly why Mal came here. The sickness is spreading, and whether it has anything to do with the Seam or not seems irrelevant at this point. It's wreaking havoc on the people of this kingdom. It's more widespread than we were led to believe. You know Mal, he commits himself to situations for the good of the people—needs no further reason than that," Fin said. He sat on the edge of his bed, letting out a heavy sigh as Yozo remained rigid, facing the window that lit him up in amber hues of sunset.

"He's different…than us," Fin slowly continued, attempting to give voice to the many thoughts he sorted through that day in the sitting room. "Perhaps that's one piece of this puzzle Lanereth overlooked. She thought the only reason he'd come here is for the possibility that this sickness has something to do with the Seam. I'm beginning to think that might have been second to the simple reason that this people, this land, is turning rotten, and it appears that no person of authority is likely to step in to do anything about it. Not the king—we've heard he's not come out of the castle walls for nearly a year now. Not the duke—we saw him last night, face paint covering signs of the warp. Nor any other neighboring kingdom. From what I've heard, Black Steel Crowns, the kingdom north of here, they've been warmongering for years with the Rediron Crowns. They're more likely to take advantage of a show of weakness than provide aid."

Fin placed his pipe and weed pouch down on top of his things, voice calming once more. "Leave it to Mal to step into something like this for the pure reason of helping a people in desperate need."

"That could be," Yozo said, opening his eyes once more. "These people most certainly need help."

Yozo put down his travel satchel, sitting on the bed across from Fin, head in hands, attempting to rub the stress from his face.

"Any leads?" Fin asked.

Yozo stilled for a moment, considering if anything he happened upon that day amounted to anything. "No," he concluded, shaking his head, knowing that the only thing he had uncovered that day was the haunting scene of Rachel and Ezel forever imprinted in his mind.

"I may have something," Fin started, still considering if it was even worth bringing up, but knowing they had little else to look into if not for this. "Fort Rediron has been abandoned for a generation or two. It's been kept empty by orders of King Maxim for some time now."

"So?" Yozo said, dropping his weary hands.

"So," Fin continued, "about a year ago, there were sightings of strange folk residing there, and the duke has cracked down on anyone from approaching the fort. Any trespassers are tried for being in league with witches."

"A year ago...," Yozo slowly said. "That's around when the warp started to surface."

Fin smiled. "Exactly."

"This group living in the fort, are they being protected by this order, or are they the ones the duke is attempting to rid the fort of in the first place?" Yozo quizzed.

"I don't know, I didn't get too much information other than that, but I think poking around the fort might be a good place to start when looking for further answers," Fin said, then added, "Either that, or it's a great way to get on the bad side of a mean duke."

"Yes, one or the other, or perhaps both," Yozo agreed.

"Likely both," Fin said with the faintest play of a mischievous grin.

Yozo stood to de-robe and gather his evening clothes, looking out the window as he dressed. The crazed man was still making the same menacing circles in the street below, the whole street corner practically abandoned now as the guards arrived with man-catchers, maneuvering to detain the delirious warper.

He wasn't often one to indulge in spirits, but tonight, he thought he'd finally take Fin up on his nightly invite to share a few drinks between them. He was ready to leave this wretched town far behind him.

Part Three: Malagar Zaval

13

PATH OF THE ROGUE

The dark gray clouds hung low just over the trees to either side of the trail as they made their way quietly down the Nightshade highway. They had seen no travelers on the road since they left the southern walls of Dunnmur early that morning. Now it was evening and the light that was able to make it through the dense cloud cover was fading fast.

"Look, the crossroads," Fin hoarsely whispered, putting them both on alert as they approached the spot in the trail where they had left Jamous many nights ago. Neither had talked of the fact that they'd need to cross that spot in the trail to get to the fort, but they had both wondered what they'd see once they arrived back to that spot where Jamous had camped.

They stalked along the roadside, eyeing cautiously the camp Jamous had inhabited days earlier. They didn't see him there, though some of his camp wares littered the area.

Fin held up a hand to Yozo, ordering him to wait

there on the road and keep an eye out as Fin slipped off the trail and into the campsite, keeping a keen eye as he searched the site for Jamous.

Yozo patiently watched the road and the surrounding woods as Fin finished up his search, returning to the road further down the trail. Fin waved Yozo over, not taking his eyes off the ground as he moved across the road.

"There was some blood there in camp. Some kind of scuffle. A day old or so, nothing too recent," Fin mumbled, still in concentration as he followed. What Yozo could now see was a trail of footprints that had been left on the previously muddy road, having dried since they were made.

The two followed the tracks as they crossed the cobblestone intersection leading westward, off towards the fort.

"I thought Jamous had been terrified of the fort. Why would he have rushed off in that direction?" Fin asked, speaking out loud.

"Look," Yozo said, breaking Fin's gaze away from the dark path in the woods leading into the Nightshade Forest. "Another pair of tracks." Yozo knelt to inspect the footprints.

"They're smaller," Fin said, kneeling beside the man. "A child's more than likely. Either Jamous was running after this kid or he was being chased by them. Jamous had mentioned something about a child. He was terrified of them."

The woods were still, Yozo's quiet voice cutting the ominous silence after a while. "Either way, they headed in the direction we are. Might as well track them while our destinations align."

"Tracking two individuals I don't wish to actually find," Fin grumbled. "Wonderful."

Padding quietly down the dark forest trail, they stalked along the road that would lead them to the fort, and likely Jamous' fate.

With the coming of a moonless night and the blanketing of fog, Fin and Yozo could do nothing but stay on the trail that led to the fort. If they had chosen to veer off the road, they knew they'd be lost within a matter of a few yards. Even on the trail, they were at times wondering if they had gotten turned around on the road and were headed back in the direction they had come.

Neither wished to bed down for the night in the eerie forest, however, and neither had brought up the suggestion to find a place to lay down and take a nap since it'd have to be on the trail itself.

They had lost Jamous' trail somewhere along the foggy path, and part of them was relieved at the thought that they were no longer heading in the direction the strange two sets of footsteps had led to.

No scuffles of predator and prey accented the deep forest night as usual, though that detail did little to surprise the two. Nothing about the woods they walked was normal. The odd malaise was all too noticeable

Yozo put a hand softly against Fin's chest, the two pausing their silent march just as a cloud of fog parted slightly, showing an open space ahead on the trail, the trees thinning out into an open field.

Yozo leaned in and whispered, "Fort could be ahead if this is the end of the forest. Should we make our approach now, or in the morning after this fog clears?"

Fin didn't get a chance to respond. The distinct clink of gear on armor as a horse galloped in their direction came into earshot, sending Fin and Yozo scrambling off the trail into one of the sparse bushes that still lined the path.

Torchlight split through the fog as two riders patrolled the edge of the forest, slowing as they came to the spot on the road Fin and Yozo had been just moments earlier.

The horses snorted in resentment for having been

yanked back and forth as the two riders paced the area for a moment, thankfully not in Fin and Yozo's direction.

"Na, it's nothin'. Probably just a deer," a gruff man's voice called out from atop the horse.

"A deer in these woods?" the other rider said, grimly chuckling as they rode slowly past them down the trail into the woods. "More warp wanderers in the west Nightshades than deer these days."

The two riders were out of sight quickly, even the light from their torches being enveloped by the fog within seconds as they rode the way Fin and Yozo had come.

The two waited patiently in the bush for the sounds of the riders to fade into the dark forest, allowing a minute or two to pass by before they ventured to untangle themselves from the twiggy mess they were in.

"This place is guarded, it seems. Better we head in now than during the day if we hope to enter that fort," Fin whispered, starting to see the silhouette of a building a ways up the trail from them.

Yozo waited for Fin to take point, slinking up the trail as the fog began to thin out.

Fin broke from the road as they neared the gates, making his way through the knee-high grass field to the left of the structure, Yozo close behind.

Approaching the wall of the old fort, they paused, listening for signs of activity on the wall above. If there were sentries patrolling the treeline, there were sure to be lookouts posted atop the wall.

A minute went by, and while they waited, they both noticed that the countryside was beginning to light up slightly, likely indicating twilight was about to come on. They needed to move fast if they were to position themselves within the walls before sunrise.

Fin raised a hand and signaled Yozo to wait where he was while Fin scoped out the stone palisade. Moving to a long section of stone covered in moss, he sought purchase along the grout and grooves of the age-pocked cobblestone palisade. Lifting himself soundlessly off the grassy floor, he quickly made his way up the twelve-foot wall, slowly looking over the other side as he hung there while peering down the parapet walkway path.

He saw no lookouts and heard no activity close by. Looking down to Yozo, he waved him to follow him up, then lifted himself over the edge, crouching on the walkway.

Yozo was up next to him just as he spotted a tree to their left that looked to be a good spot to cover their descent on the way off the wall. There were guard towers at either end that would likely offer a much easier exit with steps or ladders, but if there were guards posted anywhere along the wall that weren't actively patrolling, they'd likely be resting in there.

They moved to the bushy oak tree that leaned next to the wall and began to scale down the rough stone palisade into the fort's courtyard. They touched down behind a few shrubs just as a tower door opened, torchlight shining down into the courtyard below, giving the two a better glimpse of their surroundings.

As the footsteps sounded above, Fin and Yozo sank low into the brush, Yozo covering his face with a black scarf showing only his two dark eyes as he looked up the wall to make sure they weren't spotted while Fin scanned the overgrown courtyard before them.

The structure had not been upkept for some time, possibly several generations by the looks of it, and many sections of the exterior rooms had crumbled, exposing a few unintentional entries into the main structure. Vines wove into thick ropes, and blankets covered most of the walls and open hallways throughout most of the fort. Thankfully, Fin thought, the overgrowth was going to allow them plenty of cover to get lost in once the sun rose and burned up the rest of the morning mist.

"A month in this moldy hole is a month too long a stay if you ask me," the man atop the wall said in a hushed voice, a second pair of footsteps joining him along the narrow parapet walkway.

Without a sound, Fin placed his black cloak over his head, just as the man on the wall peered over, looking down into the courtyard. Yozo watched as the man's gaze passed over them before returning to his partner and their conversation.

"At the least if the duke gave us any reasoning behind why we went from cracking down on druggies to protecting them, it might have made this deployment a bit more manageable," the other watchman said, not as hushed as his more wary companion.

"You never know," the cautious watchman whispered back. "Perhaps knowing why we're here would have made it worse. Sometimes ignorance is bliss, my friend."

The other man had no response, and Fin and Yozo patiently waited as the two peered around from the vantage point as twilight slowly illuminated the grass fields below.

"Come on," the louder man said, breaking the silence. "Nothing out here."

Fin listened as footsteps were followed by the watchtower door closing, and they were once again lightless in the courtyard other than the faint morning glow that showed them a silhouette of the overgrowth before them.

Fin took down his cloak, easing his way over to Yozo, whispering into his ear, "Guards likely from Dunnmur. Seems they're in the dark as to why they're here. Let's try not to kill them, if possible."

Yozo nodded his agreement, before Fin asked, "What do you make of that druggie remark? Think they're harboring some kind of operation here?"

Yozo whispered back, "If so, we might want to search the lower depths first."

Fin nodded in agreement. If there was some sort of drug operation involved, even out here in the middle of nowhere, they likely wouldn't set up shop in a tower or somewhere visible at night when the torches were lit. Growers were much more cautious than that, usually. They'd find the most secluded section of this fort to set up shop.

Fin moved along the side of the wall through a patch of hedges, paying close attention to each footstep he gingerly placed as he made his way across the yard and into the outer hall.

Waving Yozo to follow, Fin spotted a few doorways leading into the outer rooms of the fort, some caved in and blocked off, only two that he could see appearing to be in functional condition.

The rain the last few days had muddied the ground, and he could see a few trails of footprints heading this way and that, and he paused a moment to wait for Yozo to catch up as well as make sense of the story the tracks told before deciding on their heading.

A few tracks disappeared behind the working doors along the open hallway they crouched in. But most, he could see, led to the end of the hall, ending at a dark tunnel entrance that looked to descend down a spiraling stairwell.

Yozo had caught up and saw what Fin had been eyeballing. Without a word spoken between them, each quietly drew their blades, Fin taking out a throwing dagger and Yozo drawing his curved short sword. The pair was the equivalent of walking death to any who had the misfortune of bumping into them down in those tunnels.

The two cloaked men made no sound as they slunk past the tunnel's threshold, entering the lower levels of the fort as the first rays of sunlight lit the mountain trees high above them.

14
CREEPING ANGEL

A faint amber glow illuminated far down the tunnel, and Fin had to tread especially carefully as they made their way through the dark to reach the first candle's light.

A dusty tall crate held a candle and a bag of apples. This was a lived-in place, it seemed, and Fin figured Yozo's hunch was likely spot-on if it was drug dealers they were dealing with. How many lived and worked down here was the real question, and why in the hells was the duke sending city guards to keep watch over it?

The hall branched into two other tunnels, with the third threshold opening up into a chamber, or antechamber. He couldn't tell how far the room went back and if the shadows playing along the walls were doorways or cracks in the subterranean structure.

He took the candle from the crate and walked into the chamber in front of them, the candle's light showing that indeed, the shadows were archways, though only going back a few feet, the multiple alcoves providing plenty of shelf space for the dwellers of the expansive cellars.

Yozo hovered over the large table in the center of the room, thumbing through the stray parchment and assortment of dirty bags, fabrics, tools, logs, and other seemingly random horticulturist litter spread out along its rough, worn surface.

Fin moved to the row of stone and wood shelving in the alcoves, finding a lab of some sort, rough flasks and corked beakers of all sizes scattered about various stations in the alcoves along the walls.

Fin rubbed his fingers together at Yozo to grab his attention, the near imperceptible sound quickly calling the perceptive man over as he abandoned the table of fertilizer and tools easily.

Fin set the candle down on one of the busier stations. He picked up a vial filled with clear liquid, giving the thing a few flicks with his finger, seeing that there was some viscosity to the liquid, indicating that the stuff was not simply water. *A sap maybe? Or perhaps something not so naturally derived?* he wondered.

Fin gingerly set down the vial, Yozo hefting a larger flask filled with more of the synthesis, giving it a swirl just as a shift and mumbling sounded from across the room in one of the shadowy alcoves.

The glassware was down and the two had weapons drawn the next moment. As a figure rolled off the bed shelf they had been resting on to have a look around, wondering why the candle they had placed in the hallway intersection was now in the room with them, Fin and Yozo crept up to the side of the archway, ready to pounce.

The woman scanned the room, her face showing signs of worry as she looked for what roused her from slumber, but she was too late. Yozo slipped in from the shadows and grabbed her, ripping her from her seat to stand as he held her from behind, blade at her throat, hand cupping hard over her mouth.

Her eyes wide with panic, breathing furiously through her nose now that her mouth was covered, she wriggled once to try and escape. Yozo allowed her one struggle, seeing how she had just come out of slumber. But one escape attempt was all he would allow her.

He pressed the blade to her neck, slitting a small, surface-level cut along her most vulnerable stretch of skin, and she instantly gave up the fight, slouching in his arms, all tension in her body giving way. Fin was worried she was about to faint, but her fluttering eyes stayed open as she pulled herself together.

Though she wore a cloth skullcap, Fin could see under the tussle of brown oily hair and ruddy complexion that the girl was young, not older than he or Yozo. Her hard lines and general lack of hygiene seemed to say to Fin that she had lived a hard life, however, and he didn't doubt that in her line of work, she'd have few qualms, if the tables were turned, slitting their throats without a second thought. He knew he'd need to watch her closely. One like her, he figured, did not go to sleep without a weapon either nearby or on them.

Best to be safe than sorry, Fin thought, putting his knife away, patting her down as Yozo held the blade sinisterly level with her throat.

He ripped her vest off, found a dagger, and patted her linen tunic down, finding another hidden blade strapped to her thigh as he swept her legs. Lifting her work dress, baring her pale, freckled thigh, he drew the blade from its sheath. All the while, her eyes were glued to him like a spider, simply waiting for the opportunity to strike. Luckily for them all, she didn't, and Fin pocketed her two blades before continuing.

"We have a few questions for you. If you don't cooperate, or if you struggle again to escape, we'll slit your throat. We clear?" Fin said, his voice cold and even as a murderer, leaving no room for a bluff. She nodded her head.

"What's your name?" Fin asked with no hint of mercy in his tone, assuring her he wasn't inquiring out of politeness.

"Agnes," she freely gave up.

"Alright, Agnes, how many others are here underground with you?" he asked.

She looked to the hallway as best she could, the blade still at her throat, threatening her if she moved too much. "Right now—three, plus me. Above though, in the upper rooms, there's two more. They come and go."

"Do they come past this room early morning? How late do they sleep?" Fin questioned.

She scrunched her eyes in thought. "What time is it now?"

"The start of sunrise," Fin answered.

"This lot sleeps later than that. Shouldn't be coming through here other than to piss, but I suspect they already done that soon after midnight," she said.

"Alright then. Very good," Fin sighed, the briefest hint of softening his harsh tone coming through. "What are you doing here? All that equipment, what's the gig?"

"We're..." She hesitated, not wanting to give up her occupation. "...growers."

Fin rubbed his brow, frustration showing a bit. "I

can see that. What are you growing and what are you doing with it? Those aren't mushroom stalls over there—you're cooking something."

"We're..." She hesitated again, only briefly this time, knowing he'd have it out of her no matter how much she didn't wish to answer him. "We're cooking creeping angel. Found a process to render it down to a potent liquid form."

"A potent form? A knife tip of creeping angel is already enough to lock a user down for a week and you're saying you're making a concentrate of that stuff?" Fin asked incredulously.

Agnes simply nodded.

Fin knew of the drug only loosely, having seen the effects of it in the slums where he grew up back in the streets of Rochata-Ung. The substance was more a poison than a drug, though that didn't stop desperate slum scum needing an escape from playing the odds on the stuff.

"Why? What does the duke have to do with all of this? Do you deliver to him?" he asked.

"No. I don't know why the duke set this up. We don't even deliver to him," she replied.

Fin's expression was one of genuine curiosity. The information she was giving was not lining up. "Then who is your buyer?"

"We run the shipments to Norburry Abbey. The duke provides protection and payment as long as the supply line is stable," she offered.

"What would happen if the supply line dried up?" he asked, probing her for what she thought of the relationship she had with her employer.

"We've never missed a delivery, so I don't know. We'd lose funding, get thrown into a dungeon in town, be tried and executed?" she honestly replied. "Your guess is as good as mine."

Fin gave the answer a moment to sink in, more for her sake than his. He wanted her to marinate on the level of trust, or lack thereof, she had with her employer.

"When's the next shipment due?" he nudged.

"We've got the batch ready over there—just finished it last night. That's why I slept out here in the lab. The others are lazy asses who apparently don't care if they get their throats slit if we run over deadline," she said, recognizing the irony of the position of Yozo's blade as she spat out her last comment.

"So, you have a good sense of self-preservation, do you? In no rush to the gallows?" Fin noted.

She didn't respond, but her sour face mocked Fin

for even asking the question.

Fin broke the silence, his tone back to a heartless interrogator. “What do you figure we’ll do with you after we’re done questioning you?”

Fin could see that Agnes was alight with thoughts, sensing the questioning was coming to a close and her next answers may very well seal her fate.

“You likely are going to kill me,” she answered flatly.

“Why?” Fin asked

He threw her off with the question, and she tersely explained the reasoning to her captor. “I might talk.”

“What if you took off with us and promised to never come back here? We’ll even pay you for showing us the way to this abbey. After we arrive, you’re free to go. No slit throats involved in that offer,” Fin proposed, hoping the girl took the proposal, though steeling himself for another soul-biting mental scar if she refused.

She thought a moment on the suggestion, asking, “Yeah, but the others will see that I’m gone. The runner was going to come down in the morning sometime to grab the goods to deliver to the abbey anyways. If you’re heading in that direction, well, the mountain pass is a canyon. We’d have to avoid him the whole time; we’d be traveling the same pass.”

“Then we had better get a head start.” Yozo spoke in a gruff voice, startling both Agnes and Fin. “Gather your shipment up for the runner as usual. If the others find out you’re missing, perhaps they will not look further than figuring you simply wanted out of the operation if all is still running uninterrupted. We may even evade a search party if they’re on a timeline, and it sounds like they are.”

Agnes thought on the formulating plan and offer for a moment before accepting. “I’ll be paid for guiding you to the abbey, and we part ways after that? No strings attached?”

“Well, one string attached. You don’t come back here and blab on us. Other than that, yes, that’s the offer,” Fin said with a smirk.

“How much for getting you through the mountains?” she ventured.

“Five gold strips,” Fin offered, no negotiation in his voice.

“Deal,” she quickly agreed, and Fin noted the slight wince as she considered if she had accepted the offer too hastily.

Fin figured the tell was a welcome sign. He needed her to be desperate, and if she truly was, she might just cooperate with them. All they really needed from her was to walk out of that fort with them without raising the alarm. After that, when they were on the road, the consequences of her attempting to backstab them came with much lower consequences.

"Deal," Fin echoed, extending a hand to her.

She spat on her hand and Yozo lowered his blade from her neck as Fin reciprocated and the pact was sealed with the claps of moist hands.

"Alright. Let's be on our way before that runner comes down here and finds us, and before the morning sun is too far over the mountain. There may still be some dusk shade to hide in if we're lucky," Fin said, allowing the woman to grab a few belongings before Yozo led them out, Fin following close behind Agnes to watch her as they made their way back up the tunnel and into the morning light.

15
MIND LOCKED

A vast expanse of light purple skies rushed by in front of him. Stars speckled the firmament, hanging high above the lavender soft mountains in the distance. He sat on the surface of a perfectly calm lake, sinking only inches into the shallow waters.

Malagar had been to that location many times during the course of his life. It was his zone of peace and enlightenment. A place that either his subconscious had made up or, perhaps, it was an actual place in space, some fold in dimensions that had been kind enough to welcome him, and only him, into.

He had come and gone from the unchanging valley in his mind without issue for much of his adult life... but now, the amethyst mountains were tinged with a crimson lining, and he was forced to fight to stay grounded on the soft, warm lakebed.

A wrinkle of pain tremored through his countenance as a throb in his head pounded through him, but he directed the flow of feelings through and past him, not allowing the pain to linger longer than it needed to be.

A second jolt slashed through his body, and before he could allow its passing, another shot through his core.

The mountains were bleeding red now, the peaceful sky growing darker, a harsh wind cutting through the valley, rushing past him.

"You can't hide from me." A wicked voice forced itself into his mind from the outside. *"I know you're in there...."*

A crush of pain along his face brought tears to his eyes, the effort to hold the valley together quickly becoming overwhelming.

He breathed deep, drawing in wells of healing in through his core.

Another snap of pain, but this time, he breathed through the sensation.

The mountains wished to be red? Then who was he to turn them another color? The sky wished to darken? Then let them be dark. The wind tore at his bare flesh? Let it be his companion then. If pain was the one feeling that was present in the now, then he would abide with it and allow it to find harbor there with him as long as it needed to stay.

Though the waves of pain continued to crash upon his body, his expression now was one of only peace.

16

ALONG THE NIGHTSHADE MOUNTAINS

The oak kindling crackled and sputtered as the three stared hypnotized into the flames that cooked the two rabbits they had snatched earlier that day.

They were all exhausted, double-timing to make sure they had stayed well ahead of the drug runner while traveling through the mountain pass. Now that they were through and on the other side of the range that overlooked the abbey grounds, they had holed up in a cove along the cliffside, which had offered them good concealment from the valley, allowing them the convenience of having a campfire for the night.

Though Fin and Yozo hadn't gotten any sleep the night before, neither had any illusions that they'd get any that night either with Agnes sharing their camp with them. It was a shame, though, knowing that if they went to investigate the abbey on the morrow, they'd be completely wiped out, and from what Agnes had told them of the place, it sounded like they would need their wits about them if they were to visit there.

“You mentioned that the abbey houses foreigners? By the way you said it, it sounded like you meant against their will. What would happen if Yozo and I were to walk up to their gates and asked to visit for a while? Abbeys are usually religious institutions. I assume they don’t discriminate against their visitors?” Fin asked, looking to the woman who eyed the roast rabbit eagerly.

“You walk up to that abbey and ask entrance, they’ll give entrance to you, but you won’t be leaving unless you’re beyond mad. Alls most anyone knows is lately, nobody visits there. Redirons are turned away, and those not local get taken in and don’t come out. Some think it’s a secret holding house to serve the king’s purposes. He has many enemies these days, many who are other kingdoms. We know best to avoid that place altogether. See how the road goes around it these days?” she said, pointing to the newer addition to the dirt road highway down in the valley below that skirted around the grounds by a mile or so. “Foreigners don’t know, though, and they get snatched up without warning. I wouldn’t go there if I were you. I don’t know what your plan was, but even Lenny, our runner, he drops the stuff off at the gate guard and heads back—he don’t even enter the walls.”

“There’s screams sometimes,” she continued after she realized Fin had no reply. “Lenny tells me that when he’s close to the gates, he can hear screams coming from within the abbey. Crazy animal noises too, like they're keeping feral beasts there within those walls. I don't know what they're doing with the concentrate we've been supplying them, but it ain't good. You don't want to go near that place, believe me."

"And yet you were helping them by growing their drugs," Yozo said, his tone more factual than captious.

"Hey, asshole, what else am I supposed to do to get by out there? I don't have a man to provide for me and I sure as hell ain't going to work in a brothel. Drugs have been the only thing that's consistently paid out," she said, idly brushing at her cut along her throat as she scolded Yozo.

"It's a harsh world out there—we understand that," Fin said, attempting to soothe the agitated woman. Though Yozo might not understand her view, Fin most certainly did. He likely shared a very similar upbringing with Agnes. No parents, on the streets, you fended for yourself, or you died face down in the gutters and got thrown out with the rest of the sewage and trash in the slums. You did what you had to do in order to survive. Drug dealing was a much lesser crime than the operations he had run. He had no room to judge Agnes, and by the looks she gave him, he thought she could feel his understanding of her lifestyle.

Agnes scowled at Yozo for a moment longer before releasing his gaze. "That's an understatement.

Rediron's gone to shit recently. All through this warp business, you think King Maxim would send decrees, have audiences with the dukes, or speak to the people, but nope. He's been holed up in his castle while the leaders, like Constantine, have gone mad and started burning people. Trade is drying up. Poverty is increasing. It's probably a good thing you two came along and forced my hand on relocating. I've been thinking of doing so for a while now, just too scared to do so till someone literally put a knife to my throat and forced me to move on it."

"You're welcome," Yozo said evenly. Agnes kicked some dirt his way, the two mutually loathing each other.

"Agnes, I only know a little about creeping angel. Knowing a bit more about that stuff might help if you wouldn't mind talking a bit about it with me," Fin said, a softness in his voice again soothing her over as she attempted to forget the brooding man sharing the campfire with them. Fin secretly shot Yozo a stern look for the man to behave.

"What do you want to know about it?" she asked, her tone softening with Fin.

"Just the basics will do," Fin replied.

"Sure. It's a mold. Not the usual street goods. In fact, very few sell it; there's plenty of other options much safer and easier to produce. The one thing creeping angel has as an edge over other options is its duration. A trip can last for days, if not weeks. The only thing is, the trip is like a trip through hell. Hallucinations are constant, the stuff stays in your system for a long time, and some users have lasting brain damage from taking too much. It's hard to grow too. Only shows up in specific conditions. Not many have a deep, damp, cool cellar like the one at the fort. To find it in the wild, you need to find the right kind of cave system. The stuff's just not practical and there's very little market for it," she said, waving her hand as if to naysay the salability of the drug further.

"Interesting," Fin crooned, considering the information, wondering why in the world the inhabitants at the abbey had need for a drug so degenerate. He logged the info, thinking to consider it at a later time to continue their conversation. He was realizing he was actually enjoying Agnes' company the past while. Yozo wasn't the most talkative travel companion, and he was beginning to feel pangs of loneliness gnawing at his corners of late.

"So," Fin said as he took the cooked rabbits off the spit, handing a portion of hare meat over to Agnes, "where do you plan to go now?"

"Likely Leniefoot or Augustine. I haven't been to either, so I won't be known there by the officials," she casually said, taking the meat, picking at it between sentences. "Who knows, maybe even head to Ishari, though I hear they're extremely hard on crime and wary of foreigners, but at least there'd be no chance of past employment catching up to me. I don't know, if the universe finally decides to pay me back for all the shit it's given me over the years, maybe I can even find an honest job there. Anything is possible, I suppose."

"Why not head up north into the Steel Crowns kingdom?" Fin asked, taking a bit of meat for himself, savoring the weeping juices as he ate.

She stopped eating, stunned by Fin's question. "You crazy? Black Steels are practically at war with us. Though there's been no official declaration, they're just waiting for an excuse to come in and conquer this kingdom. Anyone from Rediron country is taken in for questioning, and they're usually not released. We've learned long ago to not go there unless given official paperwork to enter their borders, and they don't give papers except to the merchants. They want nothing but trade from us these days."

The two men picked at their rabbit legs in silence as Agnes tentatively asked, "You guys weren't thinking of visiting there too, were you? Don't. In fact, it's none of my business, but if I were you two, I'd go back to whatever sunny land you came from and never come back, not for a good while at least. Got to be a better situation than what we have going on here, that's for damn sure."

"Not sure where we're headed after that abbey, to be honest. We'll see what we find there," Fin admitted, looking down into the quiet valley.

Agnes chewed her bone in silence, venturing to snag another leg from the spit. Neither of the men objected, and the three ate the small meal in the silence of the deepening night.

Eyes looked down from a stone perch a hundred meters away from the camp, dusty blue and black robes blending the figure in with the rocky landscape.

Dark cloth covered most of his face, and he held deathly still as he watched the three converse as the fire began to fade into embers. He knew that would allow them to see further out into the countryside, possibly even allow them to notice him now that the fire's flickering radius of light wasn't impeding their night-sight.

Many times over the past week of trailing them he wondered if he was going to need to intervene, but now with their destination clearly the abbey, they were practically going to do his job for him.

He had handed over many outsiders to the abbey warden. This time, it seems, his targets would be walking themselves into those bloodstained walls instead of at the point of his sword.

The trees along the foothills covered the lonely trail that led up to the main highway. Fin took in a deep breath of morning air, full of moisture from the morning dew, the heavy scent of grass and daisies in the field, and a dryness from the wind that blew through the gnarly oaks that rustled as they passed. It was a beautiful morning to be in the valley, and as they stepped out on the highway, a part of him was sad to let go of the gentle morning hike, knowing what lay ahead of them that day.

The road went two directions, one to his and Yozo's destination a few miles down the road to the abbey, and the other north to Leniefoot, which was a good day's travel on foot.

He took Agnes' daggers out of his pouch, admiring the pair. If there was one tool he knew and knew well, it was knives. They were nice ones, the red-handled thigh knife especially well balanced and sharp. It looked to keep an edge well. He handed them over to her.

"Watch yourself out there, Agnes. Keep those daggers close," Fin said as he held a hand out to give her something else.

She cautiously took the knives and accepted the strips of gold that clinked into her palm, her eyes widening as she saw ten gold strips stacked there.

She didn't know what to say, or even if the gold was a ruse to catch her off guard before stabbing her in the gut. She was stunned. Ten gold strips was enough to float her comfortably for a month in most any town. It was enough to actually have a real shot at getting established somewhere.

"Hope that's enough to get you that honest job you mentioned last night. It's worth it, I promise. You can make it out of the rut of your old life if I can."

She could see he was genuine, and the flood of emotions from Fin's goodwill took her off guard, tears coming fast and hot to her eyes.

Yozo turned and stepped away to give the two some space, leaning against one of the oaks by the roadside as Agnes surprised Fin by embracing him tightly.

The hug felt good, and Fin hadn't realized he had needed it as badly as he did. The Rediron kingdom had been draining, unwelcoming, and dangerous. They had been kept on their guard at every stop they made, had run long nights, without sleep, and Yozo, though he was a good friend and fierce protector and ally, trusting his life with the man—a source of positivity, he was not. The simple human touch Agnes gave him now warmed him more than he had been for much of the last month on the road. He wondered if she felt the same way.

"Thank you," she whispered, pulling herself from him, wiping her tears away, attempting to regain her composure. "You've no idea what this means."

"I might," he said with a warm smile. "Take care, Agnes."

She smiled back, taking him in for a moment, hesitating as she shared his space before deciding to turn, heading off on the road north to Leniefoot.

"*Gahh,* I wish she had gone in for the kiss...," Fin sighed aloud, watching the young woman skip up the road, Yozo rolling his eyes as he came out from under the shady tree.

"I could see it, she was *this* close," Fin jokingly said, smiling to Yozo, who relented to Fin's lighthearted insistence.

His smirk was short-lived, though, and Yozo waved Fin southward as he started walking the road to the abbey. "Come, we've spent enough time here. That abbey is a trap for foreigners. Perhaps we'll find Mal there."

The thought was sobering enough to jolt Fin back to the task at hand. If Mal was held at the abbey, every day counted. Though they had gotten very little sleep the previous nights, if any, they needed to formulate a plan to infiltrate the grounds and get some answers regarding the shipments of creeping angel and Mal.

"Alright," Fin said as he wiped his thoughts clean, steeling himself to think of only the task at hand. "It's maybe an hour walk to the abbey. Let's figure out what our entry and exit plan is."

A fresh mountain breeze blew at their backs, guiding them along the verdant valley trail as they marched along to Norburry Abbey.

17
NORBURRY ABBEY

The abbey grounds were expansive, the low wall skirting many acres of the valley countryside. Though the gray-stoned structure was not in disrepair, yellow moss and dingy roofboards showed that a groundskeeper likely hadn't been employed there for many years now.

Fin and Yozo could spot two armed men standing watch at the abbey's main gate, but other than those two, they hadn't been able to spot any other activity along the grounds or along the easily scalable walls. Fin speculated that if the rumors were true about the sinister nature of the abbey, that the lack of watchmen on the property showed that the real priority for the abbey's security was likely internal, focusing on keeping people in rather than guarding against keeping people out.

"Let's head in through that section of wall closest to the gardens. Best cover opportunity over there. From there we can scale that strut on the corner. Looks like it leads to a rooftop access or balcony. Might be a discreet way in from there," Fin whispered as the two slunk against a row of cypress bushes, scoping out the perimeter for the past hour.

"Let's just hope they don't have dogs," Yozo replied.

"Fucking dogs," Fin spat. "If I ever settle down somewhere, I'm going to get one, but damn do I hate sneaking around places that keep 'em."

Yozo ignored Fin's outburst and sat up to get a better look at a traveler heading towards the abbey along the road. Fin noticed the direction Yozo was looking and the two waited patiently as the lone man made his way to the two guards at the abbey's gate.

The figure was a way off, but they could see that when the traveler finally made it to the gate, they handed something over to the guard, and after a quick exchange of words, headed back the way they had come.

"Ah, the drug runner," Fin mumbled, watching as the man that was likely Lenny, finally arrived to deliver the shipment of creeping angel.

The guards chatted with one another for a few moments before one headed in through the abbey's main entrance, leaving the other guard there alone.

"Brown satchel, looked like," Yozo noted, still eyeing the scene.

"Yeah, looked that way," Fin agreed

A muggy breeze rolled through the grass, blowing against them as they watched Lenny disappear beyond the fields of green and the guard slump against the gate pillar, nodding off in the morning sun and fair weather.

"Well, shall we head out?" Fin asked, not particularly excited to jump headfirst into a potential hellhole of a place but knowing they likely should do so while one of the front gatemen was away from his post.

Yozo nodded, and Fin slowly got up and started to slink off through the tall grass toward the side of the abbey's walls, stopping occasionally to take in his surroundings and wait for Yozo to catch up.

The breeze was both a blessing and a curse, Fin knew, leaping over the low wall, rolling to a clump of fluffy brush. It created movement in the grass, trees, and bushes, which obscured their approach and drowned out the minute amount of sound they made as they skirted about the abbey grounds. But, if they did happen to have watchdogs, their scent was as good as broadcast through the whole garden.

They weaved through walkways and across grass, watching the front guard post as they kept watch of the row of pointed arch windows that lined the side of the building they were stalking up to. The stretch of garden grounds that they were skulking through were somewhat exposed to the structure's windows, and they hoped that no one within had happened to glimpse their approach.

Fin pressed up against the abbey's wall as he waited for Yozo to join him, and the two caught their breath as they looked to see if anyone had in fact seen them.

They held there for a minute, but no signs of anyone rushing out the abbey door to chase them down followed. They did, however, hear something deep within the abbey walls.

It was ever so faint at first, almost covered up by the rustle of the overgrowth all around them lazily swaying in the breeze, but they had had a long moment to pick out the sound, and they listened now intently on the voices screaming in agony somewhere deep within the building's walls.

"Agnes wasn't lying," Fin whispered as they sat there against the wall.

"Neither was Lenny," Yozo agreed.

Fin looked to the corner ledges. It would be an easy climb, the struts practically rigid as though they wanted to be scaled.

He rested a hand on Yozo's shoulder and squeezed. They were ragged, and he didn't know what awaited them in the sweeping cluster of buildings and wings. He didn't have a good feeling about whatever lay beyond those windows and doors, and even if Yozo didn't show it, he figured the man knew the going was possibly about to get rough.

"Let's make it out of here in one piece, alright?" Fin smiled, so delirious that his head was getting fuzzy as he tried to get through the sentence.

"In and out. It'll be a breeze," Yozo smiled back, seeing that the man could use an affirmation from him. "Now, let's get in there and find Mal and what this place has to do with the warp," he added.

The two slunk off to the side column, easily scaling it within a matter of seconds, touching down gently on the building's flat roof, heading to the balcony roof door. Fin tested the door handle, opening it with only the slightest creak, slipping in through the narrow crack, then holding it open for Yozo to follow.

The door clicked shut and the lazy morning continued as before along the garden paths, sweet aromas filling the air as the breeze playfully tousled the grass around in the fields, the sun continuing to rise high in the big blue sky.

The attic area was dim, the only light coming from the lower halls being the great windows Fin had gawked at illuminating the first floor.

They walked across rafter flooring, and no matter how careful they were with their steps, the occasional creak of floorboards threatened to betray them. With how rough the breeze outside was getting, though, their passing blended with the general creak of the entire abbey structure.

The small attic passage eventually led out into an indoor balcony, overlooking a great hall below, no doubt where many a festive gatherings had been held in years past, usually considered to be the pride and joy of abbeys like this. This great hall, however, had been neglected. Rafters were lined with old bird's nests, piles of bird droppings scattered all over the dusty tables and chairs below. Whatever it was they did at this abbey, it did not include celebration feasts.

They stayed away from the rafters, not wanting to startle the families of pigeons nesting there, eyeing the silent pair as they stalked down the stairs and to the edge of the hall's doorway.

The great hall led into a few sitting areas and rooms that looked to be offices, or record rooms judging by the few doors he saw that were open.

Fin tucked his head back from the doorway's edge as footsteps sounded, and a door opened. They waited for the footsteps to recede into the building before Fin ventured to head down the hallway that led deeper into the heart of the abbey with Yozo in tow.

The hallway came to a split, and it looked like the two branches led off into different wings of the abbey. He could hear movement and commotion further down both corridors...along with moaning and crying.

Footsteps sounded again somewhere close by, and the two fumbled into an open room just as the steps could be heard entering their hallway, someone engaged in a quiet conversation with a second passerby.

Fin and Yozo leaned against the wall, trying to get as far out of sight as they could in the crowded closet room.

Thankfully, whoever was in the hallway paid them no attention. Soon enough, there were only the sounds of screams of terror somewhere further in.

"This place is big, might take us a while to search it," Fin whispered, wondering how they were possibly going to get through the building together without being detected.

Thinking the same thing, Yozo offered, "I could search the left wing while you search the right wing. We'll get through it faster and we won't be bumping into each other as we sneak around."

Fin considered the suggestion, not sure if he was on board with it. "If you get into trouble, I won't be there to help out," he pointed out.

"It's not me I'm worried about," Yozo said, trying not to sound smug, but knowing his words were full of insinuation.

Fin almost chuckled, but he held his amusement in check, smiling at his partner. "Hell, you're probably right. You'll be just fine and I'm likely the one to find my way into trouble. I have a knack for that."

Yozo simply waited for an answer to his proposition.

"Alright. Let's do it," Fin consented after a moment. "You take the left wing, I'll take this right wing. Searching for Mal is our main priority. If he's here, we don't leave without him. Second, let's see what they're doing with that creeping angel shipment and if the abbey has any connection to the warp. If we can get out clean, let's meet back up by the row of cypress bushes we scouted at. If we exit in pursuit, let's meet up at the edge of the forest south of here, about three or four miles down off from the road. Does that sound like a plan?"

Yozo nodded, gripping Fin's shoulder, squeezing tightly in solidarity. Listening out in the hallway for a moment, he peeked around the door, then rushed off quietly down the other wing's corridor, leaving Fin there in the closet alone.

“Damn it,” Fin mouthed, tight-lipped. There was something about the place that gave him cold sweats, and now Yozo, ever reliable with his sword itching to flash bright out of its sheath, was rushing deeper into the building in the other direction. There’d be no way either would be able to know if the other was in trouble—the walls were suffocatingly thick.

You’ve been in and out of dungeons, prisons, castles, forts, crime lord compounds, a city of the dead, the list goes on. Surely you can handle yourself in an abbey, Fin inwardly chided himself.

Taking a deep breath, he listened to the sounds of the building, darting his head out. Getting a good look around, he slipped out into the hallway, rushing down the corridor, furthering the distance between him and Yozo, getting closer and closer to the cries and screams that echoed through the hellish abbey.

18

THE MAN IN GRAY

Yozo traveled under the cloistered overhangs of an inner garden gone to flower. Weeds and grass ran rampant throughout the green patch, even invading the walkways.

He quickly found a spot amongst the bushes as someone came tearing down the open hallway, cracking a whip as they went. Yozo peered out through the shrub at the man who looked nothing like a monk, his smock and trousers covered in blood as he lashed the bullwhip out across the flowering weeds. He snapped the fluff off the tops of a few, leaving glistening blood from the whip thong tips along the vegetation, a wicked smile on his face.

The man stopped in his tracks as two men entered the same outdoor hallway. The whipmaster stepped to the side right away, quaking in his boots as the two came up to him and addressed him.

The taller man, the one in plain white clergy robes, was holding a brown satchel, and Yozo wondered if that was the same as the one delivered by Lenny less than an hour ago.

The white-robed tall man looked to the whip man who hid his weapon behind his back and scolded, “Senji. I thought I told you to get rid of that useless thing!”

Senji tentatively brought forth his whip, knowing that there was now no use in trying to conceal it from his superior.

The tall man continued to chastise Senji, but Yozo paid little attention to the tiff, more interested in the man in the gray-blue cloak who accompanied the tall man.

The man had his hood up, and his face was covered by a dark kerchief. His gear looked specialized, very well suited for travel and hunting, and did not look cheap, though any commoner would not guess as much as the outfit had been comfortably worn in.

The piece that really snagged Yozo’s eye was the longsword the man wore resting along his hip. The belt, frog, and scabbard were thick, but soft suede, well layered, and stitched. The sword hilt was both elegant yet simple in shape and design. The pummel intersected in the center, housing a dazzling sapphire, one he figured alone valued the sword well above any commoner’s home in cost.

Yozo drug his eyes from the beauty, catching the last of the interaction between the two bickering men.

"Here, take this," the tall man snapped, handing over a well-smoothed wooden rod. "I've told you before, whips bleed them out too fast. A stick gives just as much pain without actively killing them. Some we need alive, and I won't have you accidentally killing the ones we're fishing information from."

Senji slobbered an apology, looking as though he were about to wet himself like a dog.

The tall man was not pacified, and he smacked the man across the head as he continued to seethe at the man. "Even if we were to use whips, use a damned nine tails and not that parlor trick of a whip, idiot. Throw that toy over the wall or else next time I see you with it, I'll be using it on *you*."

All the while, the man in the cloak stood motionless. Yozo knew the man was a trained killer. The dead eyes under the cowled hood showed no signs of amusement, pity, or anything else—this was merely another delay in his path, nothing more.

Senji was dismissed and the two parted ways, the tall man and the killer entering back into the building at the far side of the cloister. Yozo gave them a bit of a head start. He worried about the hooded one.

The wing they were in appeared to have once been

a guest parlor of sorts; dining rooms, shops or storage, bedrooms, and a commons area were now neglected and run down, and the ones that were still in use were converted into asylum-style holding cells, rough iron bars tacked onto door holes to allow for those in the hall a protected view in. Though Yozo didn't look in, he could hear the moans and cries from many of the rooms.

Though he wanted to begin searching the cells for Mal, he had to keep up with the pair of men as they traveled through the abbey wing.

Yozo watched as the two men entered a room in a better-kept section of the wing, the tall man closing the door behind them, leaving Yozo alone in the hallway. He tiptoed his way into the room adjoining the one the others had entered.

There were documents and books along shelves and a messy desk in his room, and he hoped the pair would not require anything from the room he eavesdropped from. It was a risk he would have to take.

The voices were muffled by the thick walls, but Yozo could hear the two talking, catching most of the conversation.

The clergyman had just finished up exchanging pleasantries as Yozo placed an ear to the wall, moving on to business items. "Yes, shipments have been on time and the concentrate is pure, as you can see. The liquid is clear; they seem to have perfected the rendering process. We'll test it on a few patients soon to ensure none of the potency has been lost in the process with this new version. Our contact has assured us it's even more potent, but we'll determine if that is true or not with ample testing."

"I'll let the king know directly. I'm not your usual liaison for this sort of report, but as I was in the area...," the cloaked man trailed off.

The clergyman was quick to add, "Your presence is always welcome here, Mr. White. Regardless of appointment or not, feel free to visit."

Bottles clanked together lightly during the pause in conversation before White asked, "Have you had any unusual activity on the grounds today? Spotted or subdued any intruders?"

"No. No reports of anything other than our courier coming and going. It's been a quiet morning. Why do you ask?" the clergyman inquired.

The room was silent, and Yozo was just starting to wonder if the man was whispering to the clergyman when he said, "No reason. Your drug runner must have been the one I saw on the road today."

"We have another courier coming from Sauvignon today too, just so you're aware. They're picking up the base compound for the white spice, so you may see another representative from the king on the premises if you'll still be here around supper," the clergyman helpfully added.

"No," White said shortly. "I likely will not be here then. There's one thing I need to wrap up before I leave. Do you mind if I wander the premises?"

"Surely not. Call upon me if you need anything. Other than that, I believe all keepers know you, at least by your garb, and will oblige to tend to you if called upon," concluded the clergyman.

With that, White stepped to open the door, and Yozo darted to the other wall, out of sight from the hallway.

White's boots halted at Yozo's door for a moment, the tall man held up close behind him, but the two started off down the hallway once more before turning a corner, their footfall quickly trailing off, leaving Yozo alone to consider if White knew of their presence at the abbey after the direct questioning. With one as keen looking as he, Yozo didn't doubt that if they had been spotted, White was the man that may have taken note of their skulking.

Getting up from his crouched spot in the corner of the room, he peered out the doorway. He was about to double back to investigate the prisoner cells to look for Malagar when he heard a strange growl and bark from further down the hall all the way back at the end of the wing.

If it was a dog or a wolf, he couldn't be quite sure. The hallway towards the back of the building was dim, the lack of windows making the stretch of hall unwelcoming and foreboding.

Another yip and Yozo found himself slowly pulled that way, wanting to get a quick look at what lay at the end of the hallway that made such strange sounds.

The growling trilled into yapping squeals as he got closer to the turn in the hall, and he could tell, whatever beast was caged all the way back there, was not healthy. It was not the sound of an angry animal; it was the sound of a monster that had lost its mind.

19
THE MAN IN WHITE

The once proud lay faithful section of the chapel had seen better days, Fin was sure of it. Pews had been thrown to the large room's side walls in order to make space for a rack, of all things, dried blood generously staining the table surface, rusting the iron links that had been used to restrain its victims.

"What in god's name are they doing here?" Fin breathed as he took in the horror scene, once a place of worship so desecrated.

He had seen enough to paint whoever now inhabited the abbey as the worst of wretches. If the abbey was a site of worship, then the tenants prayed to a lord of hell and not of the high heavens. Even calling it an asylum was being far too kind to its proper title. It seemed like it was more a slaughterhouse—not for animals, but for man.

One question remained, however. Why were they enslaving foreigners there? What information did they so desperately need from them; or, was information not the game? He needed answers.

A scream down the hallway brought his attention back to the task at hand. Making his way through the church, he entered the dormitory.

Moans and fanatical ramblings sounded throughout the halls as Fin snuck past room after room, hearing now that the ones screaming so loudly only did so after a bone-crushing smack across flesh. He knew the sound well from his time in and out of dungeons. He also knew that one bad crack of bone could result in death in such conditions with no treatment, and he could hear bones snapping with every blow.

Images from his youth shot through his mind. Moments of weakness—of pain. He perfected the art of lockpicking directly because of his first imprisonment. He had vowed to never be helpless like that again. The scars left on his body were the physical reminder, but the scars left on his mind ran deeper. They were resurfacing now in a flash of anger and fear.

He rushed to the cell the screams echoed from, something overriding his mind, throwing caution right out as soon as it entered his thoughts. A need to stop the one killing the victim took over. He approached the door and threw it open. He rushed in at the cowled man standing over a naked and bloodied prisoner with a bloody stick in hand. It had happened so fast that the man hadn't even noticed Fin slip up behind him.

Fin slipped an arm around the keeper's neck, locking his grip with terrible force, yanking the man over to the side of the room with such force that the man's weapon arm slammed hard against the wall, dropping the stick that had been his only means of escaping the death-grip chokehold Fin had on the man.

Fin jerked hard on the man's neck, popping it loudly, and Fin flexed his biceps so explosively that one of the man's eyeballs shot out of his socket as he feebly struggled against the violent assault.

The man's strength quickly slackened as he went limp a few seconds later. Fin held the grip firm for some time afterward, long after the lack of blood flow to the man's brain would have ensured his termination.

He flung the dead weight of the man to the side of the cell, moving to the victim cowering in the corner of the cell, arm broken and limp, half of his face swollen with an eye caved in.

The man seemed coherent still, even if his wounds were severe, if not fatal. Fin held a hand to the man, who trembled violently, vision likely clouded with his own blood, not knowing who Fin was.

"Come on, you need to leave this place," Fin said, his hand still extended. The man refused to move, still cowering in fear.

Fin turned to the keeper and yanked the key loop from the man's belt, moving back to the trembling man.

"Hey!" Fin yelled, grabbing the man, shaking him once. "I need your help. A lot of innocent people are going to get beaten to death here if you don't snap out of it and help me out."

The man stilled for a moment as if hearing Fin for the first time, rubbing his good eye clean of blood that was seeping in from his scalp.

"Here's the keys to the doors. Can you go through and open them for me?" Fin asked, recovering his temper as he handed off the keychain. "You understand?"

The man slowly nodded, looking over to the large dead man in the corner of the cell.

"We'll lock him in here for good measure," Fin said to reassure the prisoner, though he knew the man was good and dead.

He didn't resist Fin's tug as he helped him stand. Luckily, the man's legs had not been broken, and the two exited the room after strength returned to his legs.

He found the cellblock key, closing the door and locking it behind them, then looked up and down the hallway to see if any warden had heard the scuffle. It was all clear, the only sounds coming from a few moans in adjoining rooms.

"Good luck, friend. Get as many out as you can. I'll see what I can do about providing a distraction with the guards," Fin whispered, patting the man forward to get him moving.

Fin didn't wait to watch over the prisoner's progress. He knew he didn't have time to. He had just put Yozo and him on a timer before the alarm was raised, and that gave him limited time to search for Mal amongst the cells.

He rushed down the hall, looking in through the barred windows, blowing past empty rooms, some with prisoners who looked questioningly at his sudden inspection, some sure to be dead, desiccated and shrunken amidst piles of filth, some rambling and incoherent of his intrusion.

The block held many victims, but Mal was not among them, and just as he rounded the corner to the next line of cells, he saw a shadow approaching along the end of the hallway.

He slipped back to the hallway corner just in time

as footsteps came his way and stopped halfway in the hall. Keys jangled for a moment before a door creaked open, slamming shut afterwards.

Fin looked down the hallway again, finding it clear now, and began to make his way down the hall to the only room that he could hear activity in. The voice of a stern-sounding man resonated from within.

Fin nudged up close to the door, listening to the harsh man's words.

"Sorry, where were we? I had to deal with some foolishness and get a replacement *truth crier*," the man said, punctuating the last term with a slap of rod in hand. "Ah yes, your insufferable silence. We were just about to get you to speak again. It's been many days since you used those lips for anything but spewing blood. At first, I simply wanted information on where you got that Seam-smeared tooth, but now, I think I'll just break you for the completion of it. I don't often get heretics that can hold out against my treatment, but you have. I won't be able to move on until we change that."

Fin slid out a knife from his bandolier, opening the door and slipping in, mind blank but for the source of the voice, rushing the tall man in white robes just as the stick was raised to slam down on his helpless victim.

The white-robed man saw Fin and redirected his

strike at the stranger, wrath in his face as Fin slipped the blow. He thrust his dagger upwards, pounding it hilt deep into the tall man's chest, just under his sternum.

The man inhaled sharply before Fin jerked the knife out and slammed it in under the robed man's jaw, driving it straight through his skull, dropping the man instantly to the ground after the fatal blow.

Fin stood there, eyeing the dead man for a moment, vision still blurred before sound started to bleed back into his awareness. There was a commotion down the hall, as prisoners began to run past his room.

He looked back into the hallway at the emaciated prisoners who were tripping and scurrying past the room he was in. Snatching the keys on the crate by the door, he rushed out into the hallway. Grabbing the next one running past him, he slapped the keys in his startled hands, the man thinking he was one of the wardens before Fin said, "Unlock as many of these cells as you can, then hand them off and get out of here."

The trembling man nodded in obedience, still eying Fin as he went to look through the line of rooms ahead of them, finding one with a survivor in it, fumbling with the keys, attempting to unlock it.

Fin turned back to the room he had killed the man in, aware of his surroundings for the first time.

At first, he didn't recognize the man. His face was caved in, and bruises speckled his body so badly that the man's skin color was a dark purple. But after a moment, after reaching down to turn the man's face in his hand, he gasped, dropping his knife and clutching the man in an embrace.

"Mal," Fin shakily let out, hugging him tightly as Malagar bled upon him, not responding to Fin's touch.

Fin withdrew, looking for signs of life, wondering if the man was even alive as he inspected his multiple open gashes and injuries. It didn't look good, and though Fin could see Mal was alive, the beaten man showed no acknowledgment of his friend's presence.

"Mal, I'm going to get you out of here. Alright?" Fin said, clearing his voice, attempting to keep the hurt out of his voice.

"Ah, you know this one? I was the one that brought him in. He actually gave me a fair amount of trouble...," came a smooth voice from the doorway.

Fin's head snapped around to see a gray-blue cloaked man leaning on the doorframe, watching the two as another prisoner sprinted full speed down the hallway past them.

"You're creating quite a mess," the man smiled, watching the jail block begin to light up with desperate calls for help from the prisoners who were still locked behind doors.

"You know there's quite a few keepers on staff at the abbey? You likely just consigned them to a quick death," the man said as he lowered his kerchief, revealing a short-bearded face, an ugly scar down the right side of his face along his prominent cheekbone.

"A quick death would be a mercy here," Fin spat, letting go of Malagar to pick up his bloodied dagger off the floor.

The man withdrew back into the wide hallway, drawing his longsword as Fin rushed out of the room to meet the grinning scarred man.

"If you are indeed the one that brought Mal to this hellhole," Fin seethed, trying to calm himself as he finished his threat, "I'll go ahead and add a few more scars to that ugly mug of yours that you won't be able to cover up with a damned mouth cloth."

The man's smile slipped, Fin striking a nerve with him, his humor over facing Fin all but gone.

Fin was deep in a potent fury, and even with his vision slightly blurred from the rage he harbored, emotions whirling, he could tell by the man's easy stance that he needed to calm himself or risk being chopped in half the moment he blindly lunged at him.

"You...struggle with yourself," the man crooned, stepping slowly in towards Fin, Fin yielding the space.

"Ah, as I thought. You and your partner are master fighters. You know just where the edge of my reach ends with this sword. That's surely no mistake of positioning," he continued, assessing Fin's every move.

Fin too had calmed enough to begin picking apart the man's stance, his sideways positioning of his torso, taking note of his lead foot and weapon hand, how he tilted his sword tip slightly down from a raised hilt—his self-assured smile.

Fin leapt back and chucked the bloodied dagger at the man while drawing two more from his bandolier. The blade was intercepted easily by the man; the dagger clanged off his sword and flew off and into a door down the hall. The cloaked man covered the distance between them in a flash, poking at Fin's defenses briskly, snapping in and out of Fin's reach, quickly backing him down the hallway.

His enemy had the advantage, a good arm's length of certain death stretched between him and the killer. He was barely deflecting the thrusts, and he knew if he made a move to get into the man's space, Fin likely would not enter it unharmed.

The cloaked man continued his steady advance, pressing Fin to the left and then right, but always back, gaining ground as Fin lost it, edging closer and closer to the wall.

He risked one lunge, snapping the feign short to halt his opponent's advance for a moment. He flung a dagger at him, the hooded man whipping the ends of his cloak across to deflect it as he snapped in at Fin, bringing the broadside of the sword smacking across his face, spraying blood and leaving bright red lines across his cheek.

Fin stumbled back and slammed into the wall as the man advanced, thrusting for a killing blow just as Fin snapped his hidden parrying dagger free from his hip, catching the point of the sword, deflecting it to the left as he lunged forward with the dagger in his right hand.

Fin's dagger point was less than an inch away from the man's chest, but the man pulled back just in time to avoid the blow, smiling at the clever move.

"Cute, but you're the one with blood on the ground in the end," the cowled man said, barely showing any signs of exertion, while Fin was left heaving from the near-fatal assault.

Fin tightened his grip on his parrying dagger, knowing it was the only thing that stood between him and the grave.

20

SHOWDOWN IN THE CELLS

The howls of wolves could be heard down the hall, followed by screams and orders being shouted, distracting the man for a moment as he held Fin at sword point against the wall.

Footsteps were hurriedly coming towards them, and the cowled man for the first time flashed an expression of frustration Fin's way. He kicked open a cell door and backed halfway into the room so that he could chance a glance at who was rushing down the hallway towards them.

Fin chucked another dagger at the man, forcing him all the way in the room just as Yozo slowed his sprint, sword out and pointed towards the door Fin had tossed his dagger into.

Yozo slowly advanced into the room as Fin slipped by him to retrieve Malagar, looking over his shoulder once to see Yozo and the cloaked man square off in the little cell, sizing each other up quietly, touching sword tips tentatively, testing each other's defenses before either made a move.

Malagar was exactly where Fin had left him, comatose while sitting up in a meditative position. He swept in and scooped him up over his shoulder. The man was much lighter than last he had seen him... much lighter.

He hustled out of the room and heard that the racket down the hall had gotten louder, warning him that they had precious little time to linger there. He trotted over to the room the two swordsmen were in and halted in the hall, seeing the two still crossing swords, not having made their move yet.

Yozo slowly recalled his blade, the man watching with mock interest as his opponent proceeded to sheath his sword. A slight smile played on the bearded man's lips as he readied his attack on the unarmed foreigner.

White lunged in with an overhead chop. Fin saw that, though it was a simple move, it was all the cloaked man needed considering Yozo's defenseless position, and his heart sunk as the sword slashed through the air towards Yozo's collarbone.

It did not land at its intended target, however. Yozo snapped his sword out of its scabbard in a single stroke, flicking the falling sword just enough to redirect it to the side of him, slicing fabric but missing flesh. The draw had landed him to the side of the man, footwork involved in the blur of motion of the draw, and Yozo's blade slashed down quickly. He held it in place for a moment before reversing his grip on the hilt, moving to re-sheath his sword once more.

Even Fin struggled to catch the movement, and in a flash Yozo was off to the side of the man, hand on hilt once more at ready position, and the cloaked man struggled to hold his sword tip off the ground where Yozo had directed it to.

A deep line across the man's neck split open, pressure from his artery squirting thick ropes of blood off to the side as the man toppled, quickly slipping into the afterlife. He only had a second to reflect on his misjudge of the foreigner's technique, but in that second, an approving smile froze on his face as his life bled out altogether.

Yozo's hand left his sword hilt, and he quickly yanked his scarf from around him, pressing the cloth to the spurting artery.

"What are you doing?" Fin scolded, thinking Yozo was furiously at work to keep the dangerous man alive.

"Take off your clothes," Yozo ordered as he slipped the dead man's gray blue cloak off.

Fin caught Yozo's drift, carefully sat Malagar against the wall, and quickly unlooped his jerkin and gear as Yozo undressed the dead man, throwing articles of clothes in a pile next to Fin.

Growls echoed down the hallway and Yozo left the room to inspect as Fin hastily donned the other man's gear, bundling his old stuff up, shoving it into a side bag, slinging it and Malagar over his shoulder. Yozo had done a good job to keep most of the blood off of the cloaked man's clothes. Only a little wetness rubbed against his neck where Yozo had performed his surgical slice.

A gurgling in the hall hurried Fin out of the cell to see a wolf's head smack on the floor in front of him. Yozo wiped the blood from his blade on the fresh wolf carcass before sheathing his sword again, waving for Fin to follow him down the hallway.

"Put up that face scarf," Yozo ordered as they jogged down the hall. "The guards fear Mr. White. Hopefully they allow us through with you wearing his outfit. Lucky for us, he covered his face well. Here, hand Mal over to me. Act like you're leading us."

They rounded the corner and saw another rabid wolf snarling and nipping at a keeper, who cracked his bullwhip over his head, keeping the beast at bay, baton waving furiously when the animal tried to get close.

Fin directed Yozo around the scuffle, squeezing past as the keeper was shouting for help from *White*. Fin ignored the man's pleas and slipped out of the hall, the group heading into the chapel.

"Mr. White! We need your help!" another man called from the other door in the chapel leading to the other wing of the abbey. "Can't find the warden, and the patients are all over the place. Oh, and someone let the wolves out!"

The man impatiently awaited a reply, Fin patting Malagar, who was slung over Yozo's shoulder.

"Got one of them already. I'll be along soon, go on," Fin said, trying to speak as smoothly as he had heard Mr. White had.

"Please hurry," the man cautiously said as he turned to run back into the intersecting hallway.

Fin hefted a chair and threw it through one of the stained-glass windows lining the chapel walls. He grabbed a switch from the torture rack, poking it along the edges of the window to clear out the remaining shards.

"After you, Mr. White," Yozo offered, Fin gingerly making his way out of the chapel window, careful of the jagged glass all along the frame and the grass below.

Yozo hefted Malagar through the window to Fin's awaiting arms, and Yozo leapt through the frame, rolling as he hit the ground.

The two were off running across the field, jumping the low-hanging abbey wall and hustling southwards along the highway for a few miles before they slowed. The forest off to the side of the road spanned for miles, and they figured it would be a good place to get their bearings before continuing on further.

Looking back once before entering the forest, Fin was heartened to see a few escapees, naked and fleeing in various directions from the horrid place. He hoped the majority had escaped the premises, though he knew a good few likely had been detained or ravaged by the loose wolves that had mysteriously shown up in the midst of the jailbreak.

Fin carefully made his way down the mossy stones, handing Malagar off to Yozo, who stood in a small ravine with a stream running through it. Finding an overhang of slate slab, they ducked under the roots that held the small alcove together. Unless they were being tracked by dogs—or rabid wolves—they were well enough hidden from sight that Fin doubted they needed to worry about any hunters sent by the abbey. They seemed as though they had their hands full regardless, sending men out to track probably being the last thing on their minds.

"That was a lot of jostling around we just put Mal through—let's see how he's doing," Fin said, leaning over the restful man slumped against the rocky moss bed.

They didn't need to remove any clothes for inspection since he wasn't wearing any, his wounds on full display to them both. Fin gently maneuvered Malagar's legs and arms to follow long strings of bruising and inspect for broken bones. A few joints seemed compromised, but for the most part, his limbs were rigid where they needed to be. Only a few bands of muscle worried him; tendons might have been ripped from their attachment points. Malagar might just be able to walk, Fin assessed, which was good if they were going to escape from this land any time soon.

His face concerned Fin the most, however. He had been beaten so badly that Fin barely recognized him when he had first come upon him in the abbey. His skull had been practically caved in. It was a wonder the man was alive and drawing breath considering how injured he was.

Fin clenched his fist, done with his inspection, realizing the extent of the hurt that white-robed bastard had inflicted upon his friend. How long had Malagar been locked up in that hell hole?

He slammed a shaking fist into the dirt, venting his frustrations the only way he knew how at the moment, calming himself as he realized that now was not the time to lose it.

"Here, help me out," Fin said to Yozo, going to heft

Malagar's top half. "Let's get him washed off in this pool."

Yozo helped sink Malagar's lower half into the cold stream, taking a cloth from his things to gently rub away dirt and dried blood from his body. The bath helped Fin calm a bit more, as he knew that the freezing water would likely numb the hurt and reduce the swelling.

After the bath and letting him soak a bit in the crook's pool, Fin unloaded his other outfit that he had stuffed in a pouch. It was lucky he had thought to bring it as they had a very cold, naked man on their hands now.

Malagar began to shiver before he finished clothing him, which Yozo commented was a good thing. "Means he's coming back to his body," was all the explanation the quiet man gave Fin. Fin trusted him and considered it a healthy sign.

Dragging Malagar up to a bit of dirt and moss, the two laid him out once more.

"Guess we shouldn't risk a fire," Fin grumbled, looking up the ridge to the woods' edge, not thinking they'd be able to be seen from that far down in the ravine, but not wanting to risk it.

"I'll murder anyone that dares come after us," Yozo said as he gathered a few things to start a fire to warm

Malagar up with. Fin didn't bother arguing with the man. Perhaps Malagar did need the fire more than the risk of them being found. Regardless, he knew Yozo could make good on his word.

"Mal," Fin called, snapping his fingers a few times around the sleeping man's head, attempting to wake him up. "Malagar. It's us, Fin and Yozo. Are you able to give us a sign that you're in there?"

Fin opened Malagar's good eye, letting the light of the forest into a very dark place. Fin studied the dilation of his pupil.

"Malagar. Please. We need you to snap out of it," Fin pleaded. His eye remained still as he aimlessly stared off into the trees.

"Leave him be for now. His mind will wander home when it's ready," Yozo said, striking the kindling of the small wood pile he had gathered, lighting it up. "I'm glad Nomad thought to give us some ko hako. It is a good blend. It may help Malagar to wander back to us. It will ease his mind."

Digging through the pack, Yozo found the snatch of incense, taking a wad, lighting the tip until it burned bright. He placed the smoking cone on Malagar's chest, the smoke wafting up, covering the man's face.

Fin went to smell the potent aroma, but Yozo placed a gentle hand on his shoulder, shaking his head to dissuade Fin from taking in too much of the smoke.

The two sat back, sorting through their inventory of gear, attempting to see how much food and water they had on them and what survival items had made it through the last leg of their trip. They had had to ditch a trail pack before they had entered the abbey, and unfortunately, when they had left, they hadn't run across it. They had stripped down to the basics for the operation, and they counted only a few bars of compressed trail rations left on them along with two empty waterskins. The water was no issue, as the stream they were next to seemed fresh enough, but the few bars between the three of them might only last them that day and the morning.

"We'll need to restock our food supply," Fin said, stating the obvious to Yozo. "Wonder if that stream has fish in it," he wondered aloud, eyeing the patterns that played under the surface of the babbling brook.

"If there are, I'll catch a few," Yozo said, taking one of Fin's knives, grabbing some string, and heading off along the stream, leaving Fin alone with Malagar.

The day wore on, and Yozo did come back after a few hours with a line of small stream fish skewered through by a makeshift spear. That brought a smile to Fin, a sigh of relief coming to him as he now had one less thing to worry about in regards to their precarious situation.

“No sign along the highway of pursuers. I spent some time scouting there before getting to work on the fish,” Yozo said, handing the fish stack over to Fin. “With the number of wolves I let out of their kennels, I doubted they’d be doing anything the rest of the day other than staying well clear of those rabid beasts.”

Fin looked to Yozo, surprised and smiling at the admission. “You loosed the wolves? That makes more sense now.”

“They were…collecting something from the beasts. Saliva, I believe,” Yozo said, reflecting on the dark kennels. “Rabid is a good term for them. I think they were attempting to capture the essence of their sickness for some dark reason. Likely the same dark reason they need creeping angel concentrate. The man in white spoke of a courier—a representative of the king—coming from Sauvignon to pick up the base compound for the white spice.”

Fin considered the implications of that thought if it were true. Yozo added another revelation to the conundrum. “They were collecting foreigners and using them as test subjects. They must not have felt they needed much security because of how drugged and beaten they kept everyone there. Let’s hope Malagar didn’t get too many *treatments*, of the drugs at least. We can see he got plenty of treatments with the stick.”

"That...would confirm my worst suspicions. I had hoped the king had nothing to do with the warp sickness, but I fear that King Maxim may be orchestrating all of this with some compound. The question is: *Why*? Why would he do this to his people? There's nothing to gain from decimating his population," Fin said, head in hands as the weight of it all crashed into him. "How could he do this to his people?"

Yozo had no answers for him, and instead of attempting a reply, he gathered a few straight sticks, whittling the ends into points, handing them over to Fin to skewer the fish on. Staking them along the fire's edge, the two sat and listened to the crackle of wood and the trickling of the stream, reflecting on it all.

A ragged gasp for air startled the two, Malagar's eye fluttering open as he struggled for breath.

"Mal!" Fin called, holding the man's hand as Malagar began to take more ragged breaths, eye wide and attempting to focus, eventually looking at Fin.

They waited for the broken man to react, but as his eyelid sunk, he stared off at the stream, laying back along his bed of moss, breath steadying once more.

"Mal...," Fin softly spoke, wondering if the man was coherent, or forever locked in a mindless state.

"I—" Malagar choked out, his voice parched and

raw. "I hear you, Fin."

"Water," Fin whispered urgently to Yozo, who was already busy filling up one of the waterskins with water from the stream. Turning back to their comrade, Fin said, "You were out for most the day, ever since we dragged you from that place."

"Yes," was all Malagar could offer back to Fin, a sloshing waterskin being brought over as Fin helped sit him up to get a drink.

Sputtering a bit, attempting to quaff down the cool liquid, he drank deep, and after several minutes of slowly giving him drink, Yozo picked some of the crispy fish skin and meat off the stake, feeding the man little bites until Malagar sat back, satisfied.

He groaned for a time, squinting in discomfort, and they patiently waited for Malagar to volunteer when he was ready to speak with the two.

"That smoke...what is it?" he finally said.

"Ko," Yozo answered. "A...sedative of sorts."

The wedge of incense had fallen to the ground and had gone out.

"More," Malagar said, wincing through a wave of pain.

Yozo produced three more pucks of it, lighting each

of them, encircling the man in smoke as if performing a ritual. The stuff instantly made Fin's head fuzzy, and he guessed the numbing agent likely was helping Malagar get a handle on the pain.

He struggled for some time, and Yozo handed Fin two of the fishes to pick at while they sat by their writhing friend who was struggling through waves of agony. Eventually, either he was acclimating to the pain or the barrage of ko had completely overrode his pain receptors, and he settled, looking to the two men who sat by him.

"Where are we?" Malagar asked, a distant and hazy look in his eye as if he were struggling to stay focused on the two.

"Just southwest of the abbey," Fin offered.

"How...did you two find me—" Malagar started to ask, but choked up, starting to sob, tears coming to his one good eye as he lay back down along the moss bed.

It was going to be a long night, Fin thought as he looked to Yozo. At least they were there to share it with him, he thought.

21

RECOVERY AND A NEW HEADING

The golden sun basked the rocky foothills a warm tan when Malagar finally crested the last stretch of ground before they planned to stop for the night. He had insisted on walking unsupported, though his balance had given him a tough time of simply walking forward and though Fin and Yozo both had asked multiple times to help him through the rough spots on the trail.

They could tell he was in pain from the day's trek, and it had been a long one for the shape the man was in and for how much sleep, or lack thereof, he had gotten the night before. They had crossed the highway and headed into the southern Nightshade foothills to stay out of sight from any Kingsmen or abbey workers who might be traveling the road to Sauvignon. Without Malagar to slow them down, Fin likely would have opted for a more concealed route, like crossing the foothills completely and traveling through the Nightshades, but he supposed, in the end, he hadn't minded to simply skirt the highway. In truth, he could feel that both him and Yozo secretly welcomed the idea of being hunted for their trespasses, just for the chance to slaughter any monster who had anything to do with what happened to Malagar. A great deal of pent-up anger simmered just below the surface between them all.

"Come, Malagar. Camp's right up this way—we're almost there," Fin said, arm waiting to pat the man on the shoulder as he hobbled to him. Fin could see tear streaks down his swollen face as he walked with him. They walked in silence the last few minutes as they entered the camp amongst boulders Yozo had gone ahead to set up for them.

"Yozo, want to see about snaring some more of those mountain rabbits like you did last time?" Fin softly asked as he helped Malagar to his seat along a knee-high stone slab.

Without a word, Yozo disappeared into the network of boulders, either off to secure the perimeter, keep an eye along the highway miles south of them, or hunt for their dinner. Fin didn't doubt the man probably would take care of all three for them. It was truly a relief to have the man with him. To care for Malagar while keeping them safe and fed and finding fresh water sources would have been difficult at best.

"How'd you do out there on the road today, Mal?" Fin asked, hoping to get the man to use his voice a bit as he had not spoken at all that day.

Malagar remained mute, staring blankly at the ground.

Fin sighed, gently patting the man along the back, mumbling that he was there for him before getting up and tending to the campfire.

Fin had just gotten a spark to catch in the kindling when Malagar mumbled, "The Rediron warp…it's not a sickness."

Fin looked up from tending the fledgling ember smoldering along the dry bark, listening intently as Malagar attempted to continue his thought.

"The white spice. They're synthesizing some…drug —some combination. Putting it in foods for the people to consume."

Fin flamed the small fire for a moment, seeing the light taking to the twigs and branches before coming over to sit next to his companion.

"Yeah, that's what we figured. The creeping angel concentrate, the rabid strain they were milking from those wild beasts, likely other ingredients we haven't uncovered yet—"

"They were manipulating the Seam, Fin. That was one of the ingredients. That's what drew me to this land. They're playing dangerous games with the Seam that will end horribly," Malagar said, cutting off Fin before he could finish his thought.

Fin thought on the revelation for a moment. He knew very little about the Seam. He only knew Malagar was connected to the strange dimensional gateway. The very concept itself had been a point of confusion for him. He had seen others manipulate the rip in reality before, using it to blink in and out of existence, but the ability to access the fold in reality was so rare a skill that very few even knew of the phenomenon, let alone understood it enough to clearly explain it to him.

"How is the Seam involved in all of this?" Fin asked, his curiosity piqued in the conversation as it had been the one factor he had not previously considered. "The Seam is wild, uncontrollable, right? You told me it's utter chaos. No one is its master—not even the gods themselves."

"Yes, no one can master the Seam—that statement is irrefutable," Malagar said, looking into the fire, thinking hard on the mere fact of the statement.

Fin struggled with his own questions as Mal did the same.

"Then are they simply using the Seam as a wild card thrown into this deadly concoction to ensure its absolute ability to spread chaos?" Fin asked aloud, sorting through the information they had.

"Perhaps," Mal slurred, his lips still swollen. "Though I think it's more deliberate than that. The Seam cannot be controlled, but perhaps the Seam can control those who use it."

"That would imply that the Seam has a sentience to it...," Fin said, trailing off as the implication of that statement sank home.

"That it would," Malagar voiced, rubbing his bruised face in exhaustion over the long day's travel on bones that had been bound and locked up for many weeks now. "All those years in the monastery, my masters deriding my draw to the Seam because that was the one plane of the heavens or hells void of a deity. I was cast out of temples because of it. And here there may be a god deep within its folds—some cosmic horror."

Yozo came back into the camp as Malagar finished his thought, tears coming to his eyes as he said, "And from what I've seen of its handiwork these past few months...I am worried it may have been best if it never had awoken and revealed itself to the people of Una."

"The highway," Yozo tentatively said, not wanting to interrupt, "is busy this evening. There looks to be caravans and perhaps a troop of soldiers from Sauvignon. It seems word was swift about the upset at the abbey."

Fin looked to his small fire and asked, "You think we should camp fireless tonight?"

Yozo didn't answer, and Fin took the hint as he smeared the budding embers and flames across the dirt before there could be too much smoke at its snuffing.

"Likely no meat tonight anyways. I'll see what else I can forage," Yozo said, bounding off through the boulders once more before Fin could reply.

"Mal, who is at the head of all of this? Someone's orchestrating it. King Maxim is likely involved. There're too many signs to not suspect that. Duke Constantine's involvement, soldiers at the fort and representatives at the abbey, Mr. White's involvement. Yozo mentioned he was reporting directly to the king on production and shipments and bringing foreigners with too many questions into the abbey for detainment." Fin noted the wince at the mere mention of the man who likely had history with Malagar according to White's own admissions to Fin in their fight. "If it's the king at the head of all of this… I just don't understand the motive of doing this to his own people. What am I missing?"

Malagar looked at the man struggling with questions he didn't have answers to and offered, "I'm not entirely convinced all of this is just the king's doing. The man you killed in my cell—the white-robed man…" Malagar halted as he mentioned the man who had ruined his body and mind thoroughly. "I have seen white robes elsewhere in this kingdom."

Fin's eyes widened, realizing the multiple places he had noticed the ambiguous sightings of those robed figures—patrolling in Sauvignon, flanking the duke in Dunnmur, at the head of the abbey; he had even seen a few in Tarrolaine, though it was a small hamlet of a town. He had considered them just some religious sect known to the region. It was a new land to him. He had no reason to think of them as anything but that, but the more he considered their presence, the more he thought back through his memory, even before entering the kingdom.

He had seen similar garb in the Southern Sands, his homeland—in the streets of Brigganden. They had shot his friend, Terra, in the chest with a bolt…. His mind raced with the need to understand the connections.

Those zealots worshiped some false god. They had professed they worshiped the god Elendium, but his friend Terra had said they followed a false shade of what they thought was the benevolent god. There had been no chance to obtain the truth of the matter as Elendium, through Terra as his conduit, had purged the heretics on the spot. What if there was a connection between that cult and the white cloaks here in the Rediron kingdom, and how was the Seam involved with it all?

This new god...could it be the shade Terra had guessed at? Zealots unknowingly following a false version of the god they thought they were faithful to?

His mind whirled with the speculations and possible revelations. Malagar had not been there to witness the cult of Brigganden. They would have slipped his suspicions, but they—if it was in fact the same cult—were visible to him now.

"Perhaps they mean to manipulate the king," Fin said of the cult.

"Perhaps King Maxim means to manipulate the white robes," Malagar countered, "or perhaps the Seam means to manipulate *both*. It's anyone's guess at this point."

"Indeed. I suppose we don't have enough information on any of them to come to firm conclusions at this point, or what their endgame is," Fin said, taking Malagar's point.

The two sat in silence, reflecting alone with their thoughts until Yozo came back into camp, handing out seeds and a few gooseberries, which they made quick work of. Alone, the meager meal was not enough for Malagar, Fin thought, and he broke half a trail bar for the man, offering up the last of one of the waterskins to him to go with it. Malagar didn't refuse the extra portion.

The sun set quickly over the grassy plains, and Malagar was out before twilight began to darken the sky, completely exhausted from the day's exertions, leaving Fin and Yozo up to organize and plan for the following day's hike.

"Come," Yozo said, motioning for Fin to follow him to perch up atop the set of boulders that protected their camp from view.

Fin was settling down along the slope next to Yozo as Yozo admitted, "I overheard your conversation with Mal. This kingdom is already in a bad way, and it seems the real horror has only just begun for these people. Many will suffer in the coming days..."

Fin looked over the beautiful landscape, only the faintest light from a caravan far to the west any indication that they weren't alone sharing the vastness of the Rediron countryside, taking in the view.

"Mal needs us," Fin whispered, looking upon the beaten-down man resting below along the rocks, understanding what Yozo was hinting at. They could not afford to step into this mess of a situation now with Malagar as bad off as he was.

"He needs one of us," Yozo said, looking to Fin.

He felt Yozo's eyes on him as he looked over the sleeping man. Yozo was right. One of them likely would be enough to handle the injured man and extract him from the hostile kingdom, back to Canopy Glen or beyond. He was sure James, the farmer they had stayed with, would put them up for a time while they nursed Malagar back to health. The man was kindhearted.

"You suggesting we get involved here?" Fin asked, finally meeting Yozo's firm gaze.

"I...have not slept one night without that girl's screams echoing in my mind," Yozo said, and though Fin did not know what girl he was talking about, Yozo having never mentioned his visit to Jamous' family, Fin could tell by the man's solemn expression that whatever travesty he had witnessed had fundamentally influenced him.

"Someone needs to pay for what they have done, and what they are about to do. The innocent have no power to do anything about the wrongs being committed in this land. The system they live under is conspiring to poison them, and they are generally innocent to the schemes that are sealing their fate. If we don't step in, I fear no other will," Yozo finished, and Fin could hear the resolve in the man's voice, as though he had already made his decision to root out the systemic scheme, with or without Fin's help.

"I feel Malagar is our first priority. He has suffered a great deal. I'm not sure he'll ever get over those scars given to him in that abbey. Mal needs out of this kingdom—now.

"I agree," Yozo readily said.

"As to which of us is to extract him and which is going to continue this investigation...I have a say on that point." Fin paused for a moment. He knew Yozo would not like what he had to say, and he knew there would be some convincing to get the man on board with his plan.

"You're better on the road than I am, and in duels, but you don't trump me in every area. My gift is the voice and shadows. I grew up and survived by talking my way out of tough situations. I know how to get information, how to slip past officials, to not be seen by those I don't wish to be seen by. I've been in and out of castles and keeps more than you have. It looks like the evidence of who's behind all of this is pointing to King Maxim. I'm our best bet at getting in those walls and getting some answers. I'm a bit tanner than most in these lands, it's true, but with White's outfit, I can cover up that fact well enough. White was about the same height and build as me. You're shorter, have a heavy accent, and with your slanted eyes, if anyone looks under that hood, they are sure to see through the deception."

Yozo seemed ready to interrupt Fin through his whole speech, and yet once Fin paused, Yozo had nothing to say, thinking over their situation more thoroughly. Fin could only offer the man a few final words on the matter.

"I know you want to go after this lot, probably worse than even I do, but I'm our better play, and you're more likely to get Mal back to Canopy Glen with fewer hiccups."

Yozo finally looked to Malagar, the man twitching as if in pain in his sleep. Pulling out a puck of ko, he jumped down from the boulder, landing softly. Searching through the smear of embers from the defaulted fire, he found a coal and lit the incense from it. He placed the smoking stack next to the man's face, waiting, watching for a time until a calmness finally settled over his bruised features.

"Fin," Yozo said in a low voice as to not wake Malagar. Fin looked to the man, waiting for his travel partner to speak.

Yozo's eyes did not leave Malagar as he said, "You had better not fail. I will not forgive you if you made the wrong choice in our roles this night."

Fin looked upon the man, quiet now, no further words needed to convey the stark reality of the zero-sum game they had stepped into—that *he* had just stepped into. Yozo understood the cost of failure, and he was forcing Fin to appreciate what was at stake.

He would do what it took to bring those responsible for the warp's spread to justice, even if it led back to the king himself. And since there seemed to be no justice to haul the perpetrators to for sentencing, he would have to substitute as jury, judge, and executioner.

Part Four: Castle Sauvignon

22

ALONG THE FLOODPLAINS OF SAUVIGNON

The bit of soap Fin had washed the clothes with only minimally helped to rub out the bloodstains along the cloak and vest top of White's outfit. Fin supposed it could have been worse. Yozo had prevented the clothes from being completely ruined by the amount of blood that spurted from the man. And if Fin had cleaned the outfit overly so, he wondered if the men he was about to report to the following day would have believed that he had been out on the trail at all. Some degree of unkemptness seemed to best suit the circumstances, and if he was going to impersonate the tracker, he needed to consider all the small details surrounding him.

He had talked with Yozo at length about what he knew about White, which was, admittedly, very little. He had told him of a few speech patterns the man seemed to favor, as well as describing the direct connection the man had with the king, but that was most of the usable information granted. Malagar likely knew the most about the killer...but Fin had not thought the information worth opening up such a freshly horrific memory of the one that had delivered him to his captors.

He dipped the cloak again in the small stream along the outer reaches of the Sauvignon sprawling town and farmland. He'd camp there on the outer reaches of the town for one more night before heading in to settle the matter. It had been far too long since he had a full night's rest, and what he headed into would demand him at his utmost. He needed all his wits about him when he made his move. A great deal rode on his performance.

He threw the gray-blue cloak over a tree branch to dry overnight. The spotty cleaning would have to do. Though the nights were getting a bit colder over the last few days, even without his cloak that night to warm him, White's travel garb was well suited for the winter nights.

He was growing rather attached to the inherited threads, very much approving of the craftsmanship of the set. It added a good deal of padded protection and warmth, but wasn't overly bulky or restrictive. White had fended off his daggers well with the sturdy cloak, not a cut showing in the fabric, though it had done nothing at all to help protect him against Yozo's surgical blade. He knew nothing short of plate armor would have shielded against an attack like that, though even then, Yozo likely would have found a gap somewhere in the suit.

He wasn't the best with swords though, and he had brought, perhaps at a risk of being found out, his vanishing dueling dagger. He lashed it to his belt on the opposing hip from White's longsword. Aside from that, he stuck in a throwing knife along his vest for good measure. Even though it was near impossible for others to get a good glimpse of it in the open, it did imprint under the cloak slightly. Hopefully if any did happen to notice the bump along his hip, they'd think nothing of it. In the end, he felt wearing the trick of a weapon was well worth the likely paranoid risk he fretted over.

He laid back along the grassy knoll, looking out over the quiet countryside. It was a peaceful land, aside from the systemic injustice being secretly administered by those in power. It was a shame they had seen the absolute worst of the region. In past years, he wondered if it would have been a wonderful change from the baking deserts of Tarigannie.

He had changed since his humble beginnings in the desert region. He had met good people with an extraordinary amount of respectable character. Being in their presence and fighting a united cause had shifted his own morals, slowly but surely.

It all had started with Reza. A young, naive saren expecting to change the world for good. And somehow, against every ounce of cynicism he could muster, she had outlasted him with a seemingly endless amount of passion and drive, and they had ended up playing a large part in fighting back the tides of evil that nearly enveloped the Southern Sands Region.

It wasn't *just* Reza that had softened his outlook on life–Matt, Bede, Nomad, and others had played their part in living for more than just himself–but Reza was the center of most of it. He wondered, without her, if the group he had come to know and love, would simply disband and drift their separate ways. She was their rock–the glue that bound their fates together.

She had taught him that occasionally there were causes worth fighting tooth and nail for. Some things were bigger than even one's own survival. A commitment at that level seemed to be the only way those big world-changing efforts ever seemed to come to pass.

He supposed that's exactly why he was about to do what he was about to do. He was prepared to give his life to stop things from getting worse—whatever it took.

He smiled, consciously giving up the hope and expectation of survival. Fear and worry faded from his aching joints. He'd be better off without allocating a large portion of his focus to self-preservation, and he couldn't allow anything to get in the way of the success of this mission.

He closed his eyes, letting the sounds of the night critters chirp and croak as they willed, allowing the exhaustion he had been putting off for the past week to finally overtake him, sinking him into a deep slumber.

23
THE QUIET ROAD

Leaves blew down the forest trail, pressing against the two men's cloaks that had been drawn up close to keep the chill from their bones as the winter breeze blew across the highway. The highway patrol thought nothing of the passing couple as they did the same, cinching their hoods tight to keep the cutting wind from freezing their noses.

Yozo and Malagar silently thanked the rough weather and chill of the higher altitude as they passed their second patrol that day. They assumed that they were on the run from officials, though doubtful as it was since the news of their exploits at the abbey had yet to travel all the way to patrolmen between Tarrolaine and Canopy Glen; still, they wished to remain as safe and anonymous as possible given their foreign complexions.

Malagar's swelling had gone down greatly, and even his skin had begun to flush out the bruising, though it had turned him a sickly yellowish green throughout much of his visible skin. Though it looked grotesque,

Yozo knew it to be a good sign of his recovery.

Once again, they were alone on the road, endlessly walking along the paved path eastwards. Yozo supposed many would have found the long days of hiking from sunrise to sunset a burden and a thing to grumble all day about, but he had found the quiet woodland trail a welcome reprieve from the bustling streets and oversight of Sauvignon and Dunnmur. The steady pace and repetitive motions had been therapeutic to the mind and offered hours of both reflection and introspection. He could not be sure, but he thought Malagar felt similarly.

"Yozo," Malagar said after the patrolmen had long disappeared from sight, breaking the day's silence between the two. "You...wish to remain in Rediron, don't you? I can make my way back to Jeenyre Monastery. I do not wish to be a burden on you—"

Yozo cut him off, a slight tinge of frustration in his voice. "—You are a burden to no one, Malagar. I stay by your side because I *wish* to, not because I *have* to. I only wish I had hunted you down with more urgency than I had—"

This time, Malagar was the one to cut in. "—Don't you dare blame yourself for what happened to me back there. I got myself into that mess. It's my own damn fault I did not leave Lanereth with more information about my whereabouts. I didn't want her hunting after me, though it seems you all didn't let that stop you. Had I known how much trouble I'd be to you all, I would have been more frank with her about my suspicions."

Yozo let the comment simmer for a moment before acknowledging, "I suppose we cannot blame ourselves for any of this. No one could have known what threat lurked in this land until we saw it for ourselves."

Malagar stopped, wincing as he held his left side. They had stopped a few times in the last couple of days for the snag in his hip. It had not allowed him as leisurely a hike as Yozo had had.

Yozo fished out the last ko from the pouch Nomad had tossed him and Fin. He thought twice before stuffing it back in. The night was always the worst of the man's pain. At least he'd have one more night without waking every hour in screaming fits.

"More will share my fate, Yozo," Malagar said, offhandedly voicing the dread that had been on his mind that whole day through the miles of road.

Yozo came to his side, supporting him as he worked through the spur of pain that was locking up his hip.

"Fin will make sure they don't," Yozo said, more confidence in the statement than Malagar had heard in a long while.

Malagar's leg painfully unlocked, and he shook off the painful strain of muscle as he started to limp along the trail with Yozo helping him along.

The wind had died down, and the highland road rounded the bend to present the two with an overlook of Canopy Glen miles off in the valley far below. It'd be well into the night by the time they arrived at James's farm, but he'd push them that last day to ensure that he got Mal fed and slept in a warm bed. His companion earned himself a long season of rest.

With Malagar's arm slung over his neck, he considered his own season ahead of him as they slowly made their way down the trail. He still had many miles to go, he knew. Many sleepless nights along stretches of road lay between him and his allies who hunted down an entity that remained a mystery to them. It might be the case, he thought, that the force they chased after might very well end up being too much for them to handle, even if Reza and Nomad had fought, and defeated devils in the past.

He wondered if they had walked into the same danger that Malagar had unwittingly walked into. He would not find sleep until he confirmed their safety.

His firm gaze was set not on the town ahead of them, but on the highway that led from it to Alumin.

24

DANTE WHITE'S RETURN

Conversations died off when he rounded the block, eyes magnetized to him as murmurings floated just out of his earshot. The tracker's notable reputation, Fin saw, was undisputed. The man was either respected or feared throughout the whole town, likely a mix of both.

He was adjusting his cloth mask and hood when he just about ran into a city guard coming out of a side street. The man profusely apologized, instantly recognizing the outfit.

"Mr. White! Ah, terribly sorry. Almost bumped right into you."

Fin straightened, not expecting to be put on the spot so soon into the city borders, but ready to put his rehearsed impression to the test.

"Don't worry about it," he tested, watching the man from under the hood carefully to judge his reaction.

The man seemed grateful he had not caught

the tracker on a bad day, smiling before recalling something. "Ah, yes. The Marshal wanted to see you as soon as you were back in town. He's actually on shift somewhere around the outer gate. You might catch him if you hurry. Evening's wearing long; might be turning in for the night soon, or be off dropping in on other posts. He likes to do that."

Fin smiled under his veil at the small victory. He had fooled one guard at the least.

"Take me to him," he smoothly commanded, no room for argument in his voice.

The guard hesitated momentarily, but nodded and replied, "Sure thing, Mr. White. We'll track him down," then chuckled slightly at the irony of the comment.

Luckily, the guard either wasn't interested or brave enough to talk much at Fin. For the most part, Fin focused on memorizing the street network and layout as they weaved through town towards the castle, which loomed clearly above all the buildings below it. The small hill the castle sat on gave it a picturesque positioning from the town's view below, with the backdrop of low-hanging brooding clouds and evergreens and tall hills behind it, giving it the appearance of a castle straight out of a fairytale storybook.

The castle walls stood oppressively to either side of the road ahead, and the guard shouted out to a guard posted out front, asking where the marshal was. They were pointed within the castle walls as the man called in through the gate, the wicket opening for the two to enter. The two passed through the threshold and the door closed loudly behind them. Fin beat back the feeling of entrapment that his intuition was warning him of, walking with the same saunter of command that he had seen White exhibit.

Great oak trees canopied over them as they entered one of many inner courtyards, the guard continuing to ask passersby where they could find the marshal.

He was just about to call off the search, wondering if visiting such a high-ranking officer was wise. Likely White would have been well known to the higher-ups. He might be playing his cards too aggressively right from the start. Just as that thought had come to him, the guard let out a relieved breath and announced, "Ah, there he is, Marshal Reid. Should have guessed he'd be here. He always talks to the guards posted in his court block before he heads off shift. Cares greatly for the servicemen, he does. Wonderful leader."

Fin looked to the man the guard now waved to. "There you are, Marshal, sir. Mr. White and I have been looking for you. Thought for a second there you'd gone and just disappeared on us!"

The guard had called to a man in a faded green trench coat casually smoking a thin cigar that was speaking with a watchman on duty. The comment halted him mid-conversation, and he turned to Fin.

"Mr. White," the man called, and Fin recognized the man as the same who had bought them a meal at the pub in town so many evenings ago.

"You're filthy," he tersely said, his tone not a pleasant one as he regarded Fin. He tapped his cigar ash, his whole demeanor a picture of dislike for Fin's cover, White. "Do you wish to get washed up before we talk? I've been waiting for a report from you for days now."

"Now is best," Fin said coolly, glad that the man had given him the option. If he thought his skin tone was due to trail grit, all the better.

"Fine," the man obliged, saying a few words of parting to the guard he had been chatting with, waving Fin over as he led him through the courtyard and up the court's stairwell to the second-story rooms.

Reid walked down the balcony to the only room on that side of the court, producing a key and opening the hardwood door. Flicking the spent cigar butt over the balcony, he motioned for Fin to enter and shut the door behind them.

Fin looked around the room, finding the quarters to befit that of a high-ranking officer like Reid. He smiled under his mask. Knowing where Reid slept was a good first location to discover, one that would likely cost Reid later, Fin thought.

"So, what came of following those two foreigners —the man with the daggers and the quiet one?" Reid asked as he turned to the window, drawing back the curtain for the last rays of sunlight to filter through the thick panes of glass.

Fin held open his cloak and slipped out one of his throwing daggers, flicking it across the room to thud as it stuck into the side table Reid stood next to.

Reid's eyes were wide for a moment. He regained his calm quickly as he caught Fin's drift, plucking the dagger from the wood and inspecting it as he answered, "I see. Well before you poke any more holes in my furniture tonight, a simple 'they were taken care of' will suffice."

Fin shifted, hoping the move was within White's character. He folded his arms, sighing in mock boredom as he awaited Reid's next move.

"There was an upset at the abbey a few days ago. You know anything about that?" Reid probed.

"No," Fin answered with measured hesitance, attempting to portray mild surprise at the news. "I was in Dunnmur most of last week."

Fin watched the marshal's features, attempting to gauge how well he was pulling off White's voice.

So far, Reid seemed to accept it, though he noted pauses between their conversation that worried him slightly. It could simply be Reid sorting through the information Fin was giving him, but part of him worried Reid was analyzing him, feeling something was not quite right about the tracker.

"Well, there are reports, and they're all early, mind you, but reports describing a mass escape of the patients there. Some of the animal subjects were loosed too. We sent a platoon there to clean things up and conduct an official investigation."

Reid paused again, and Fin chanced an interjection. "So, what, you want me to look into it?"

Reid waved his hand, dispersing with the suggestion, turning to look at Fin directly.

"Dante," Reid said, his voice a shade more dire, "I... worry that what the king is engaged in is...not for the betterment of the kingdom. In fact, I feel he's involving himself with some very dangerous allies who are actively working at tearing this kingdom apart."

Reid eyed Fin like a hawk, attempting to see through his mask and hood, trying to assess how he was taking the information. It seemed to Fin that Reid was more worried about how White was receiving his doubts in the king's ability to rule than if Dante White was in fact Dante White.

Fin moved over to the window, sharing the view with Reid, looking out into the shadows of the courtyard, two guards holding dutifully at attention down below as they kept watch of the block.

He was glad Reid had his own unrelated worries within their conversation. The more he worried about his own skin, the less attention he'd spend assessing the off mannerisms Fin was undoubtedly showing. He had not studied White long enough to perfectly emulate the man, he knew with certainty. It was only a matter of time before someone called his bluff, and any little trick to delay that moment helped extend his time.

"You...doubt the king's judgment?" Fin whispered as he continued to watch the dying light on the horizon.

Reid held still for a moment, the silence in the room all-encompassing. He sat in his armchair in a huff, not happy with where the conversation was headed.

"I am loyal to our king, you know that. I've upkept his orders thus far—"

"—But how much farther?" Fin interjected, keeping his voice a whisper.

Reid began to crack, Fin could tell, even without looking at the man. Treason was no small claim, and they were skirting dangerous subjects for a high-ranking officer to be even entertaining such ideas, especially to a man who, according to Yozo, had regular dealings with the king.

"The king requested your presence upon your return. You should go see him," Reid said, his tone cold and terse now.

Fin did not wish to oversee his welcome. He likely would not get much more out of the man after his undertoned threat anyways. After a moment, he turned to go, opening the door.

Reid eyed him closely as he left, the shadows of the early night still playfully dancing with the last glimmers of twilight along his brow and eyes. Heading out of the room, closing the marshal's door behind him, he left the second-story walkway and wandered the block, looking for a guard on duty.

The castle grounds were impressive, well kept, and well-guarded. He entered the main walkway and made his way over to a watchman.

"Is the king in the throne room?" Fin casually asked, hand comfortably resting on the hilt of his sword at his hip.

"Should be, sir," the man replied.

"Accompany me there," Fin ordered, waiting for the man to lead first.

"Uh, sure thing," the officer replied, slightly put off by the sudden distraction to his shift. He set his polearm to the side of the stone wall he was stationed at, then headed off to lead Fin along the road that led to the castle proper.

Fin walked in silence, though his mind was awhirl with noise. Thoughts, tidbits of information that might or might not be relevant to his act, and possible situations as he approached the king all bombarded his mind as he attempted to formulate a plan of action for what he was going to say and do once in front of the king.

He wondered if White was better known to the king than to the marshal. Generally, he'd place his bet on the two servicemen having a tighter connection, but he had heard the way Reid had spoken guardedly to him. Even if the two were peers in status, it did not mean they were destined to like each other and be close. In fact, often that fact made higher-ups enemies. The game of status often got vicious at the top.

He had not liked the look Reid had given him as he was walking out the door. The man's expression had gone from concealed worry to calculating. Something had happened between Fin's threat and his leaving to change the man's mood, and that was not good. At the least, he thought, he was out of the man's presence. He had kept up the farce for one visit, but chancing a second encounter with the marshal would be dubious at best.

If the king knew White better than Reid, then he would soon be approaching the main test of his persona mask. He would have to be ready to fight or flee on a moment's notice. Often a king or authority figure with that much power would have a special sign to indicate for his guards to seize or kill the man in question. He would have to be attentive to the king's gestures. Even a glance to a particular guard could mean death to the one in audience with the king.

The walkway to the castle's great hall was lined with ice-blue flowers; the species, Fin could not place. Their aroma seeped through even his mask, a crisp sweetness filling the air around the main doors of the hall. The guard went to open one of the large doors, getting the okay from the two guards standing post there.

The great door opened, granting a view of the king's hall. Extravagant rose windows let in the cool light of the green moon, illuminating the throne from behind, while torchlight warmly lit the pointed half staircase that led up to the king's royal sitting area.

The guard who had accompanied him bowed and saw himself out, heading back to his post, leaving Fin alone to take a slow step forward. He made his way across the carpeted entrance past the king's guard that lined the sides of the room, watching Fin closely.

Two spearmen lowered their shafts, holding Fin at the midway point as they waited for the signal from the king to allow Fin access to come closer.

Fin could feel the two guards' eyes on his, and he was keenly aware of White's slightly lighter eye color. He hoped it wasn't enough to tip off the guard who likely saw them often. He could do nothing about it if it was, so he kept his gaze fixed on the king ahead of him.

The king was attired in stately red satin and velvet, his coat, tunic, and trousers threaded and trimmed in a dark gray. He filled in his outfit well, and though he was not a large man, Fin could see he had a defined figure under the tailored cut of fabric. It was likely the man knew combat judging by his figure, and if Fin did make a move to assassinate the king later, he knew he'd have to strike fast and competently, or risk missing his opportunity.

"Dante, come." The king casually waved the man over as he proceeded to look through documents along his worktable that was positioned in front of the throne.

Fin bowed and came forward as the king put down the notes, snapping a finger to a guard. That produced a cold sweat from Fin for a moment, before he realized the two guards were hastening to either side of the king's table, lifting it and placing it to the side of the room so that the king had no distractions in front of him while he talked with his trusted agent.

Fin stepped up to the lowest step at the foot of the throne space. The king had not seen his first bow, and to be safe, he bowed again, adding a greeting this time. "My king."

The man's face was as Fin imagined it would be: a stern face, hard lines and brow, unforgiving and exacting. He studied Fin for a moment before speaking.

"I suppose you've heard of the mess at the abbey?" the king asked.

Fin nodded in affirmation.

"This is a most inopportune development, especially at a time like this. Elise may be...*displeased* with this news. And it would not do to have our closest ally unsure of our reliability at this time."

The king closed his eyes, steepling his fingers as he talked. He waited, perhaps in thought, and Fin was about to speak when he continued, rubbing his temple. "I have sent a platoon to clean things up there, but I would like you to follow and oversee that our operations are secure and reinstated. Is that clear?"

Fin bowed slightly, more to muffle his reply than to sell his respect, "Yes, sire."

Fin waited as the king further deliberated. He had not yet been dismissed, and so, he knew the king had something else to discuss with him. His stomach churned with nervous acids as the king kept silent eye contact with him.

"Marshal James Reid," the king said at long last. "What do you make of the man's loyalty?"

Fin noticed the cautious lead into the subject. It seemed the king wished to have his honest opinion before he said more on the matter.

Fin cleared his throat. "You may know this, but Reid and I have been at odds for some time."

The king chuckled lightly, murmuring in reply, "You don't say."

Emboldened that he had played his cards well, he continued, "He's on the fence with what we're doing with production."

The king sobered at the comment and asked, "He knows of production?"

"He's a smart man—he has figured out most of it." Fin paused, only for a moment, to consider if he should take the chance to probe the king on the subject. "What...part of the operation most concerns you that he might know about?"

The king, as Fin noticed he had a habit of doing, contemplated his response in silence, in no rush to produce an answer to his servant. The king looked to the guards and waved a hand to them. Fin involuntarily swallowed, his throat bone dry, as the guards moved past him and, thankfully, left the room.

The king was silent as they waited for the doors to be closed behind the guards, and Fin considered briefly if he should attempt the assassination right then and there. Though they were the only ones in the room, he knew the guards were waiting just on the other side of the door. He likely would stand little chance at escaping afterwards. Not only that, but the king was still a few strides away from him. If he was a competent fighter in the least, he could likely hold Fin off as he called for the guards.

Perhaps there was another reason he felt the moment was ripe for taking the man's life. There were still so many unanswered questions as to why the king was taking part in such an insane scheme in the first place, along with discovering who was helping him carry out the destructive plot.

The king continued once the guard had withdrawn from the room. "It does not matter how much he has come to learn. I have reason to believe...that he may not be fit for service once the next shipment of white spice is sent throughout the kingdom. The kingdom will suffer a crippling blow, and the Black Steels have been prepared by the Torchbearers of TenbrizLux to take advantage of our supposed weakness. Everything that ensues thereafter will require that I only keep company with those I can trust to remain faithful to our cause. Unless you have information to advise me otherwise, I wish to employ your services to remove the marshal from his position tonight before you head to the abbey on the morrow."

Fin found himself genuinely shocked by the king's call for assassination. The marshal had seemed duty bound and loyal, though the more he considered the situation, he did feel the marshal seemed more loyal to the health of the kingdom than the insane path the king was on.

"It shall be done, my lord," Fin said with another bow, thinking to add one stipulation. "If you could, sire, grant one request to aid my work?"

"What is that?" the king asked.

"Could you order the night watch in his courtyard lobby off? Perhaps find them another post this night?" Fin asked, still bowed.

"That...may look suspicious," the king said, rubbing his beard.

Fin nervously waited the king out.

"Though I do plan to visit with the priestess Elise tonight in the chapel. I suppose it wouldn't be too out of place to request further security of the perimeter," the king said, ruminating on the proposal.

"Very well, the block will be cleared," he said at last, adding, "That is all."

Fin came out of his bow and turned to leave.

"And Dante," the king threw in just as Fin was about to the door.

"If you succeed with this task tonight, be ready for a promotion," the king said, his growing smile troubling Fin more than it should.

25
THE QUIET COURT BLOCK

He turned the corner to his courtyard, looking around for the guard who usually was posted along the west corner of the block. Though the torch was lit, Taylor was not standing under it like he usually did at that time of the night.

Perhaps taking a piss, Reid thought, looking up to his window on the second floor, seeing a warm glow from within. He had left a candle or two going. He had considered lighting a fire in the hearth tonight and wind down with a brandy, but that had been before he had talked with the officers who had taken the report from the abbey keepers. Now, he only needed to change out of his evening wear and back into his shift uniform—he had the feeling tonight was going to be a long one.

He had not gotten a good feeling about Dante's answers earlier. There had been something *off* about the whole encounter. Heading to the captain who had spoken with the abbey workers that had taken the initial reports, he had asked if White had been mentioned at all, feeling it odd timing for the man to finally show up just when they were having a crisis on their hands. Sure enough, the captain said White had been mentioned in the report, though no further details could be gleaned other than the keeper who had given the report had mentioned White was there earlier, just before the jailbreak.

Dante had either lied to him or…

He skipped up the stairwell, feeling the urgency to gather his things and track White down pressing upon him. He had not liked the man's tone upon leaving his room earlier. He didn't like any of it.

He slipped his house key from his pocket, unlocking the door hastily and entering the welcoming room. He was heading to his bedroom when he slowed to a halt. There was someone else in the room, he could feel it.

Sure enough, he heard the creak of the floorboard across the room behind him. He must have seen the shadowy figure in his periphery upon entry, well hidden, but to his trained eye, telling.

He lunged for the old display sword mounted on the wall. It was his father's old military saber. The blade held many nicks, but the blade would still cut. Pivoting quickly, he turned to face his foe.

"White," the marshal spat as Fin calmly took down

his hood and mask as he walked towards the man.

"Not White," Fin admitted, stepping into the candlelight.

"You...," Reid said, shocked to see the foreigner he had conversed with at the pub all those days ago. What had the man's name been? Fin?

"If I had been White, you would be lying dead on the floor now," Fin said, standing within Reid's reach, though holding no weapon.

"I could kill you here and now," Reid threatened, stepping even closer to the man, sword point only inches from Fin's undefended midsection.

Fin held his hands wide in a gesture of surrender. "You could, but if you do, be prepared to watch the king completely annihilate this kingdom unchecked."

Reid studied the man's face, his posture. The man seemed to be genuine. Fin was completely at his mercy, sword point hovering along Fin's sternum.

"What did you do with Dante?" Reid asked.

"My friend killed him at the abbey. I've been taking on his persona," Fin answered.

"Murdered a servant of the king," Reid sneered.

"It was self-defense. White was there to kill us," Fin

corrected, adding, "and we would not have been his only hit jobs of late. The king, thinking I was White, just ordered me to kill you this very night."

Reid scoffed. "I highly doubt that. I've been serving him faithfully my whole life, and my father before me."

"Reid," Fin sighed. "I only know the king from my interaction with him tonight, but he made it clear of the direction he is heading with this kingdom, and he knows you are not on board with his course. He's made up his mind about you. You have no future with him in this kingdom."

He had seen changes in the king over the last year or so, all bad ones. He had served the man, Hugh Maxim II, with honor his whole life, and his father servicing the king's father before them. A two-generation line of loyal service had been established, and as much as he had not wanted to even consider what Fin was telling him to be true, he knew that the king had been delving into dangerous things with the council of Elise. The church's influence had been a terrible blow to the king's judgment, by Reid's estimate.

Fin's suggestion that the king was nearing a conclusion to his service was a distasteful thought, but one he had worrying notions of for some time. It was the nightmare he refused to allow any headspace to.

He lowered his sword and flatly said, “Out with it then. Why are you here?”

Fin lowered his arms, taking slow steps to Reid’s bar, having a seat as he helped himself to the brandy bottle and a glass that was out on the center counter.

“Hope you don’t mind. I haven’t had a drink for a long time.”

The man seemed tired as he uncorked the bottle, and though he had not shown it in his voice, Reid knew fatigue, and he knew the man was beginning to flag.

He allowed him the drink, or at least didn’t object as the man took a swallow of the strong liquor.

“King Maxim means to poison the entire kingdom, Reid. From what I’ve gathered, he’s produced, and about to distribute, a shipment of white spice that will cripple if not outright kill the majority of the Rediron Crown’s villages, cities, and towns. He told me that he’s made a deal with the church to lead the Black Steels to believe now is the time to strike the Rediron countryside to overtake it, which they will, if the shipments illicit the results I think they will. Why he would agree to set up his own kingdom for his enemies to take it is still beyond me, though. I don’t know exactly what his plan is past that point.”

Reid passed by the man, grabbing a glass himself

and pouring a splash of brandy. "Why tell me this? I'm the king's marshal. Don't you think I'm going to do as I should—have you arrested and tried for treason?"

Fin smiled; a confident smile, Reid noted. "You don't seem like that kind of man. This is a gamble, I know. You have the opportunity, and right, to run me through right here. Call it a hunch, but the way the king talked about you...well, he made it sound like you'd be likely the only person in any position of power to actually do something about this catastrophe that's about to happen. I believe you serve the people of this kingdom more than you serve the king himself when it comes down to it. Tell me, am I wrong?"

Reid gritted his teeth at what the man was saying. He had to admit, he liked Fin as White much more than he had liked White as White. But what Fin was leading to was to admit his king, whom he had served and been faithful to his whole life, was irredeemable and on a path that needed to be stopped. The only likely way of stopping him at that point was to kill him, and regicide was not on the table, not for him at least.

He threw back the shot and thought on it all for a bit, pouring another drink. "If what you are saying is true, I'm a dead man standing, the kingdom is doomed, and the king has lost his mind. That's a lot to take on faith, pal."

Fin nodded. "Yes, it is. Though it's not just hinging on my word. You likely know of the drug operations at Fort Rediron, and the manufacturing efforts housed at Norburry. The shipments of white spice have been shipping from here in Sauvignon. An acute man like yourself likely has looked into the stuff, if not found out for yourself what the spice really is. You've seen the effects of the Rediron warp. It's coming from the spice! A mixture of creeping angel, rabid animal strains, and laced with Seam residue somehow. I've never seen such a devastating mixture of shit.

"It's been labeled to the populous as a rare spice, up-class stuff. So far, it's only been shipped out in small quantities, just enough for the market to eat it up and inflate its value. I hear the stuff tastes good, but the warp conditions come on too slow to correlate it with warp sickness, and the people more than anything have sought after it just because it's the new thing and is hard to get. What happens when the king sends wagons full of that poison to each hamlet in the entire kingdom? Everyone is going to eat that stuff up."

Fin took a final swig of the liquor and hung his head for a moment, letting the fumes of the strong drink relax him before continuing. "From the sounds of it, the king has been cold on you for some time now. Likely you've seen the signs of that here and there. You notice there's no guards posted around your block tonight? The king pulled them from their watch so that I could get a clean kill, no witnesses or interference."

Reid had seen the signs, which was why he had been so worried about the tone of their conversation earlier when he had thought Fin had been White. The king was not himself lately, and he worried he'd be replaced sooner or later, or given an order he would refuse to obey. And he had his suspicions about the white spice. When he had first confronted the king about it, he had been told it was a humanitarian operation and that no further investigation or questioning would be permitted by any officers, including Reid.

"What's your proposal then? What was the point in telling me all this?" Reid grumbled, conflicted in the conversation he was having with the fugitive.

"Well, Marshal, is there any higher ranking than you in the Rediron military?" Fin asked, eyeing Reid as he finished off his drink.

"Nope, I'm top of the line. Only the dukes hold similar power, but they're a civilian office, I'm military," Reid said, folding his arms, returning Fin's stare.

"Well then, if something unfortunate were to happen to the king tonight, what would happen to the politics in the kingdom—who would take over?"

"I don't like where' you're headed...," Reid said

warningly.

"If something isn't done to stop the king, thousands will die, the kingdom will be overrun and sacked, and you will have no kingdom to protect and serve, Marshal," Fin replied, restating his question. "Now who would take the crown if the king were killed tonight?"

Reid rubbed his eyes, thinking on the question a moment before replying. "The king has no family. It's a dead family tree; not even distant relatives in power. I would step in as retainer until the dukes made claim to the crown. We'd have a gathering of the town officials in the region and come to a conclusion during a conference on who would take the throne. Not many would have a very clear path to it, though. Duke Lufairer Constantine would have been, but since the death of his wife and his madness, the only other viable options with enough governing experience and popularity would be Duke Carmichael from Leniefoot or Augustine, or myself."

"Good," Fin said, meeting Reid's eyes as he admitted, "I don't know much about you, but I know you at the minimum care about the people of the kingdom to some degree. There might be upheaval and tiffs amongst the dukes, but that, I'm hoping, is a better outcome than poisoning the whole damn populous."

Reid sighed. "And what of the church? This all

started upon their showing up. Elise has embedded her white-robed zealots throughout the kingdom uncontested. Somehow they got their hooks in the king, and he's waved all restrictions to them. He's been listening to her council more than his own court. Even if he is removed, she will still remain, and perhaps that's even worse than it is now. Her influence is downplayed. We could unearth something terrible by uprooting the structure."

"Yes, I've considered that," Fin said as he stood up from the stool. "He's actually going to be visiting with her tonight at the chapel soon. That's where I'll make my move. If I can, I'll take care of them both."

"I can't believe I'm even considering this," Reid sneered. "You're speaking of regicide, Fin. Hugh has served his people well for decades! Is there no other way to resolve things here?"

"You tell me. I'm doing the thing I was trained to do. Kill. If there's any tricks you have up your sleeve to solve this peaceably, by all means. But if we don't end this tonight, that shipment is going to be sent throughout the entire kingdom, and the blood of an entire kingdom will be on our hands for not intervening," Fin replied.

There was no other path that Reid could see as viable. Fin got up to leave the room. As he reached for the door handle to go, Reid called to him. "Fin. I won't be a part of a plot to kill my king. I'm sorry. But I won't stop you from doing what you think is right—for this night only. If I ever see you again, I will do my duty as a man of the law."

Fin held at the door for a moment and answered, "That's all I need from you. If I succeed tonight, all you need to worry about is taking the crown and ruling as a bare-minimum, passable king. You'll never see me again after tonight."

With that, the man exited into the courtyard, the frosty night air seeping into his room before the door was closed behind him, leaving Reid alone at his bar with two empty brandy glasses.

26
THE WOUNDS THAT REMAIN

The dying light across the western mountainside took with it the remaining warmth that was left from the slightly cloudy day. The skies seemed heavy with bluster, and Yozo could feel a chill blowing in from the east. Their first real winter storm might be on the horizon.

The good farmer James had been kind enough to take them back in. This time, Yozo had insisted on them paying him for the stay. Malagar was in bad shape, and he had required quite a few things from the town's general store. James had sent his son there with Yozo's coin to fetch fresh linens, curative ointments, and some specific herbs, seeds, and roots that Yozo planned to use on Malagar medicinally, as well as to make more ko with. The list had not been short, but the boy had come back late that afternoon with all that Yozo had asked for.

Scooping up a bucket of ice water from the stream, he returned to the house. There were still many preparations to keep him busy the rest of the night. Ko was no simple recipe, and creating a binding solution and setting them out to dry overnight would take some time, and Malagar needed to be stripped so that he could properly clean and set his wounds. Some were deep…worse than he could heal himself.

He passed James on the way in the house, bowing once again to the man. He had agreed to allow Yozo and Malagar the small house to themselves for the evening as Yozo tended to the man's wounds. The farmer and his boy had set themselves up a temporary bedroom in the barn. Yozo had added an extra gold to their fees for the inconvenience and had to practically argue with James over accepting the tip.

"Malagar," Yozo called to the man who languidly shifted on the bed, trying to rouse from his restless nap. Perhaps, Yozo thought, it would be best to come back to him after his medicinal concoctions were prepared.

He went to the table with all the supplies the boy had picked up for him in town and started to take inventory, separating out categories of items to begin making a batch of ko. Malagar's groan had him deciding that beginning the ko first would likely be a good place to start with the night's tasks.

Even though he had thought to leave Malagar with the farmer, in Malagar's state, Yozo did not think he could ask that of James or Malagar. His friend needed medical attention, and he didn't trust to leave him with anyone else in town in case whatever trouble Fin was managing to get himself into had repercussions to them as well. Canopy Glen was still in Rediron country, even if it was on the border.

Malagar's best chance for a speedy recovery was back at Jeenyre Monastery, where they had come from. Lanereth was the most skilled healer he knew, and she also had a strong friendship with the man. Yozo knew he'd have a good rest there...he just did not wish to lose the time in taking him down there since he worried for Reza and Nomad, who were likely up in Alumin, possibly poking around in the same wasp nest that they had poked. If possible, he wished to keep Reza and Nomad from being stung like Malagar had.

A jolt of pain caused Malagar to seize up, wincing as he squirmed in the bed to try and relieve the pain. Yozo had wished for the pain reliever drugs to be ready before he performed his inspection, cleaning, and bandaging of his friend, but he worried that if he waited too long, Malagar wouldn't have the energy to withstand the torture of setting joints and bones late into the night.

He sighed, steadying himself for what was to come. The night would be long, and he was glad for the farmers' sakes that they had decided to leave the building. They would have gotten no sleep that night if they had not.

He began a soft chant, a meditative mantra, clapping his hands together and rubbing them until they were hot with friction, then he threw back Malagar's coverings and began a massage to prep Malagar's body for the mending process.

It didn't take long before he knew the trail to Jeenyre was a necessity rather than an annoyingly prudent option. Malagar had seen too much abuse for him or likely anyone in Canopy Glen to fix. The only ones who could help the broken man now were the sarens.

27

THE CHURCH

The light blue moonlight from the larger of Una's moons, Phosen, lit the night castlescape for Fin as he skulked through the narrow wedges of space between buildings that clustered the corner of the eastern castle wall.

There were fewer guards along that quadrant of the castle grounds, possibly since it was the least used section of castle, the library and chapel taking up the majority of that space, but also likely due to the reshuffling of guards Fin had convinced the king to call for. He could tell when he came across block guards that they seemed distracted, or unfamiliar with their beat that night. He was glad he had asked for the shuffle; it'd make his job much easier.

The castle's chapel was impressive to say the least. Though it was not nearly the largest worship house he had ever seen, the skill and precision of the architecture was simply gorgeous. Flying buttresses delicately supported the geometric arched domes of the inner cathedral room, small towers off-shooting from various sections of its internals, supported on both ends with a stout block of rooms that Fin assumed to be the foyer and the funeral chapel.

The yellow-gray stonework seemed smooth, and they would give him trouble in scaling them, but the green tile room looked very well upkept. Once he made his way onto the roof, he should have very little trouble finding a door, window, or embrasure to slip in through.

The king's guard was stationed at the door, three of them at least. Fin suspected that the other three he had seen in the throne room were along the perimeter somewhere. A few extra castle guards, likely the ones that he had asked to be reposted from Reid's wing, were along the paths to the chapel, but Fin could tell they were staying out of the king's guard's way.

He didn't know how long the king was going to be attending the chapel with the cult leader. He needed to move faster than he would have liked to. Picking a side of the church wall with no entrances ground level, he made his way across the cloister orchard garden, thankful for the blooming vegetation and ample cover for him to slip behind as he made his way to the building's wall.

One of the city guards down the street was starting to light torches along the path. It was at once both an annoyance and a relief. If they were still lighting the area, the king likely had arrived not that long ago and planned to stay long, but it also put him on the clock to get out of the garden and up the church wall while it was still dark in the area.

Looking both ways along the chapel wall one last time, he ran up to one of the buttresses, climbing it along its underside, clambering up to the strut that connected it to the main dome of the building. He ran across the bridge of stone, hoping that the narrow line of blocks would hold his weight, and found not a single tremble of protest from the solid construction as he bridged the gap. He was along the church's line of windows quickly after, looking for an easy way in.

The windows were not hinged and couldn't be opened as far as he could see, but the dark embrasure openings below the slope of roof he was walking along would do nicely.

He dropped down along the roof's edge, swinging in through the tight opening, and climbed down the inside ledge. He touched down in a dark, quiet chapel room.

28

PLANS UNFURLED

"Something's not right," a gravelly-throated woman whispered, as she lit another candle within the domed center room in the chapel.

"The abbey incident was a minor setback—if that. We already have enough white spice produced and stored to distribute to most of the kingdom," the king said, waiting at the altar at the head of the long chapel.

"I've been having premonitions of late. Our god is trying to tell me something—warn me of someone," Elise murmured, thinking out loud. "They could be connected to the abbey incident. What do you know about the break-in?"

"I'm sending White there first thing tomorrow, and a platoon is already headed there to conduct a full investigation. The abbey keepers that came and broke the news to us seemed quite confused over the order of events. We'll get to the bottom of it, though—no need to worry," the king assured the priestess, keeping as cool a demeanor as he could.

Along the balcony overlooking the church rites circle, Fin crept soundlessly closer to the overhanging seating area closest to the stage the king and priestess were presently in. As he came up to the pillared railing overlooking the couple, he stopped to listen to the ongoing conversation. Luckily, whatever the subject of interest was, it was too sensitive to allow guards in the chapel. Even members of the king's personal guard were not present.

"It should not matter at this point. As I mentioned, we have enough white spice to poison most of the kingdom. It will be more than enough for you to convince the Black Steel Crowns to see our weakened state and suggest an invasion. Our countryside will easily be overthrown."

"What of the strength of your military here in Sauvignon? You will still need to be able to defend yourself against the brunt of the Black Steel army," Elise said, probing the king's preparations and tactics. "Even if they're slipped white spice, it will take some time to cripple their organization. We will ensure the queen and all lords in their homeland are assassinated, but they will not leave their homeland defenseless. You will be required to have a force sufficient to launch a counter-campaign upon Castle Blackrock, which will be defended to some extent."

"Yes, we are retaining the majority of military here in Sauvignon these days. I've sent word to Leniefoot and Dunnmur that there is to be a draft of able-bodied men in the following weeks. We're recruiting slowly over that period of time. Also, word will be sent to all military and nobility that there will be a knight's festival," the king explained, watching the priestess closely as she finished lighting the last of the candles.

"We're promoting the festival to be the biggest event the kingdom has seen in many years. We should have a great number of our forces and potential forces housed here in Sauvignon, retained safely away from the invasion. We'll send supply caravans to support the failing cities, all filled with a great deal of white spice during the invasion. At that point, it will only be a matter of time before the Black Steel army starts to feel overleveraged when word of their queen and lords' deaths reach them and they're deep into the stores of white spice. We'll sweep in with our main force, capture them, and head straight to Castle Blackrock to take it.

"Both kingdoms will be ours within the close of the year, and you will have my loyalty as you continue to build your god's church here in the Crowned Kingdoms. From there, we need only the support of the Golden and Silver Crowns."

She slowly walked to the center of the room, meeting the king across the altar and confirmed, "The church will handle the extermination of all people of import in the Black Steel Crowns kingdom. Their army will have no support once they're in your territory."

He gave Elise a hard look, attempting to drill home the importance of her commitment to the operation. "The timing of events will need to be executed flawlessly. We'll need to coordinate succinctly with both of our forces to pull off the campaign."

"You needn't worry about our dependability. We will help facilitate negotiations with the remaining Black Steel dukes after their castle and their army has been dealt with. It is in both our best interests that both nations have a speedy recovery after this is all over," she said, her patience with the king's persistent questioning starting to annoy her. "As long as you mandate our religion as the sole religion in your kingdoms, we will continue to support and ensure that you remain king of your people."

The king nodded. "You have my word that Umbraz shall be the only god our people worship."

Fin's worries had been verified. It seemed that the king indeed was selling out his people, using them as pawns in a game of power and territorial control. Two kingdoms were about to be plunged into a very brutal and devastating war, and the people that were going to be hurt the most were the innocent countrymen and women, all because a cult wanted to increase their congregation and because a greedy king saw a path forward that would allow him to reign over two kingdoms instead of one.

He needed to stop this diabolical plan dead in its tracks that night, or a great many lives were about to be thrown on the pyre of the king's unquenchable flames of aspiration.

With no guards present, the assassination seemed straightforward enough. The tricky part would be getting out of the chapel if either one of them managed to scream loud enough to alert those outside of the building. He would have to strike fast and silence both within moments of each other.

He drew his vanishing dagger and gripped White's longsword and crouched, ready to spring from the balcony. His fabric made the slightest of sounds when he got into position, and the two at the altar quieted and turned, looking into the dark chapel as they heard the movement.

Fin needed to make his move now or risk being seen. He leaped over the balcony, throwing his vanishing dagger at the cult leader while unsheathing his longsword, ready to rush at the king once he touched down.

The dagger would have hit dead in Elise's chest if she had not thrown her arms up just before the blade hit its target, slicing through her arm with ease, knocking her down to the floor.

Fin landed and rolled, coming up in a sprint

towards the king, sword in hand, covering the gap between the two in a flash. His sword point thrusted in at the king's center but was deflected last second as the king parried it to the side with a quickdraw of a sidearm.

Fin pressed the king back against the altar, quickly overpowering him with prods and slashes. The king threw his night cloak in front of the blade to attempt to deflect Fin's thrust, but Fin circled the maneuver and brought the point back to center, thrusting the tip straight into the man's neck, retrieving it quickly, spinning around the altar to slash at the priestess.

Elise had gotten up and recovered her wits, though, and she pulled a long, ceremonial dagger from the folds of her white robes and blocked the blade, falling back behind a statue in the center of the room.

The king fell, his dagger clanged next to him on the marble floor as he slumped, clutching his opened throat. Blood gushed forth, and though he tried to scream, nothing but a horrific gurgle came out. He lay face down as he went still, a pool of blood quickly covering the spot he lay on.

Fin scooped up the king's dagger and chased after the priestess. She was almost to the chapel door when the king's arming dagger thudded deep into her back, dropping her hard on the cold stone floor.

He looked to the king, quite certain that if the king

was not dead now, he would be within moments. He dashed to the priestess, aiming to finish her off before making his escape.

Reaching down, he roughly turned her over to get clear access to her vitals to deliver a clean killing blow. A flourish of shining colors flashed from her eyes, startling Fin for a moment, just long enough for the priestess to slip her ceremonial knife blade through Fin's defenses, stabbing him in the side.

The sharp pain spurred him back on his heels to get him out of her range, but the thrust had been her last reserves of energy before succumbing to the mortal blow of the dagger that was lodged in her back.

She fell to the floor, her eyes still glowing with brilliant flashes of color, and as she exhaled her last breath, a nova of iridescent light shot forth through the room, knocking Fin to the ground. He clutched his bleeding side as he watched waves of light flood out from the motionless robed woman.

In a flash, a message had passed through him, a discordant voice of warning washing over him—a message loud and clear, but without words. The twisted moaning and creaking of the dimensional ruptures and shifts pushed Fin's mind to the brink, threatening to rip his sanity from him the longer the jarring chaos wave rattled out along the bright nova. The message was more a feeling than anything–indelible and frightful. *Beware those who oppose me.*

Fin was dazed, head spinning and side hurting, but he knew he had to act fast. He wasn't sure how far the strange burst of light had traveled, but he doubted that the church walls had stopped the strange blast. Guards would be in there within moments.

He got up, clutching his side, and bent over to yank his vanishing dagger from the dead priestess, sheathing it with a crisp snap at his side. He grabbed a snatch of his cloak and pressed it to his side as he took off towards the doorway the priestess had been running to. He knew he wasn't going to be able to lift himself and swing his way through the arrow slit he had entered through.

He pushed open the door, closing it behind him, and started down the stained-glass hallway that led off into other parts of the church. He was halfway to the door when he heard someone approach it at the end of the hallway.

He dashed into one of the side halls, leaning tight against the inset frame of a window as two of the king's guards sprinted past, rushing into the room he had just left. The door violently jangled on its hinges as it smacked against the wall and rebounded shut, which Fin was grateful for. He caught a glimpse of a convergence of guards rushing from both chapel entrances to their slain king. He needed to get as far away from the crime scene as possible.

He exited the church through the doors the guards had come through, and as he snuck his way through the shadows of the castle yards, attempting to remain conscious as he clutched his bleeding side, he began to hear the rolling cry of alarm.

"The king is dead! The king is dead!"

29

BEFORE THE MORNING SUN

"Look, the priestess' blade," one of the king's guard said, picking up the ceremonial knife that was next to her. "I had seen her with this knife before...it's bloodied."

"And the king's dagger remains lodged in her back," another of the six king's guards announced.

Reid had been called forth, and he had shown up quicker than the guard had expected. He walked the scene, remaining silent as the others scoured the room and building for evidence of any others present.

The marshal made his way to the chapel's back door and eyed the door handle. The scene suggested that the priestess had stabbed the king in the throat and that the king, in his last moment, had thrown his dagger and killed his assassin before she could escape. If that was all true...what was blood doing on the door handle leading to the chapel's exit?

He discreetly wiped the blood from the knob with his cloak, then went back to the others and announced his verdict.

"You all know that the king had not been acting himself since the arrival of Elise and her god. I fear what we see here tonight may be the result of the white robes attempts at controlling this kingdom. I fear...Elise has killed our king," he declared, leaving no room from the others to give voice to doubt of his verdict. "The king's guards are Kingsguard no longer. You are knights of the realm singularly now until and if we reinstate a new king. Until then, you follow my orders—is that agreed upon?"

Some hesitated a moment, the edict coming quickly, but all six nodded their heads in agreement.

"We have a long night ahead of us," Reid said, looking to one of the knights. "Sir Renton. Gather some of the castle guard and see to our king's body. Wake the mortician and king's doctor. There's no question from the look of it that our lord is indeed dead, but we should confirm that fact with the court doctor. We'll then need our mortician to begin preserving his holiness's body quickly before putrefaction sets too deeply in. The people will want to see him one last time, and he needs to be in as kind of a light as possible. Is that clear?"

"Yes, sir," the knight said, saluting and heading out of the chapel.

"Sir Brexton, see to this traitor's body," he said with

a sneer towards the priestess's corpse.

"The rest of you, split up and decide who should tend to our announcements, both to our service men and women and to the people of Sauvignon. We'll also need someone to see to rounding up Elise's followers. We have some questioning to do.

"Understood," they replied, each getting busy with their respective tasks, a few castle guardsmen being led in to start the first watch over the crime scene as people came and went.

Reid had been out giving orders and overseeing the situation as it unfolded, eventually returning home a few hours before sunrise. He knew the next day was going to be another long day of speeches, public messaging, sending off representatives throughout the kingdom to declare the news, structural reorganization…he needed at least a few hours of rest before the heavy lifting of the fallout of the king's death really took flight.

On his way back through the castle grounds through dark streets, his thoughts drifted to Hugh Maxim. He had known the king his whole life, and though not casual friends, he had shared many an evening in the man's presence, and he liked to think that the king had appreciated the years Reid had spent in servitude to him, ensuring the safety of the kingdom. Over the last year or so, the respect the king had had for Reid's service had waned. It was a pity things had ended how they had, but Reid had little time now to linger on sentiment. The kingdom demanded his full attention.

He practically dragged himself up the stairs to his room on the second floor, his boots heavy as he made his way to his quarters.

Taking a thin cigar out of his jacket pocket, he lit it from the flame of a sconce, taking a relief-filled draw before letting the smoke seep out from his lips. He looked over the court block, blowing another stream of smoke out into the dark of the night before turning to head the rest of the way to his door.

He went to unlock it but found it slightly open. Pushing it open, drawing his sword, he entered at the ready.

He came in to see a disheveled Fin, his skin flush, his skin tone now about as light as White's actual hue.

"You lost blood tonight, it seems. Not surprising—I saw your handiwork in the chapel. Was that your blood on the back door?" Reid quietly said, closing the door behind him, lowering his sword, though still keeping it out.

Fin gave Reid a hard look for a moment, taking a swig from the bottle of brandy that was uncorked once more.

"You knew of this scheme Maxim was involved in,

at least to a degree—enough to be liable in my book. I'm not happy about that," Fin growled, for a moment making Reid glad he had not put away his sword.

Fin corked the bottle and threw it in his travel bag, cinching it closed before throwing it over his shoulder, wincing through pain as he did so.

"You alone know that it was I who killed the king, not the white cloaks—but they might as well had. They corrupted your king," he spoke as he walked towards Reid, whose sword raised to make some space between them. "He was about to sell out this kingdom. The harm he would have thrust upon this people would have been unprecedented."

"I did not know about the specifics of the white spice—" Reid started.

Fin cut him off. "—The hell you did."

Fin eyed the man, Reid's sword tip gently pressed against Fin's chest. "With your rank, you have great influence of where this kingdom goes next. Right what wrongs your king was tangled up in. Break up the abbey. Disassemble all white spice production and distribution. Expunge all cult influences in your domain, and never open relations with this *Umbraz* again. If you don't...I will come back here and I will see that you lay face down in a pool of your own blood—just like your king."

Fin lingered for a moment, allowing the threat to sink in before putting up the hood of his damp cloak, freshly washed of blood.

"Good day, Marshal," he said, opening the door, adding before leaving out into the court, "Don't give me a reason to see that you should share your king's fate."

He sheathed his sword, stunned for a moment, absorbing the foreigner's words, hardly knowing him, while at the same time feeling like he knew more about Fin, and the kind of man he was, than most under his own command. He stepped out onto the balcony, looking out into the courtyard. Fin was nowhere in sight.

The morning sun was about to rise. He had not gotten any sleep, and he doubted after that encounter he was going to.

He closed his eyes, putting a hand over his face, letting out a deep sigh. His king was dead, his kingdom was suffering, and the stability of Rediron had not been in such a weakened state during his lifetime.

It was going to be a long day.

30
LISTLESS SURRENDER

"Fin, this looks bad. How did this happen?" Farmer James asked, holding up Fin's shirt to inspect the blood-crusted, rough-stitched cut along his side. "And who the hell stitched this for you?"

"I did," Fin chuckled, which caused him to wince from the pain. "And you don't want to know how this happened, believe me."

James eyed the scoundrel hard, and for a fleeting moment, Fin actually felt guilty that he led such a dangerous lifestyle. That quickly passed as he thought about the potential humanitarian disaster he had prevented. Sometimes it was worth living fast and hard. James likely would not approve of what he and his friends were tangled up in, but *someone* needed to handle that stuff, and he'd be lying if he didn't occasionally enjoy living that life...when it didn't involve getting stabbed in the gut.

"Well, whaddya think?" Fin asked, sucking in a sharp breath as James gently pressed the surrounding areas to see how the stitches were holding up.

James stared at the weeping wound and said, "Well, you're not septic, which is good. If your gut had been sliced open, you wouldn't have made it this far. But you need to see a doctor. I can have Jim run to town and have the town's doc here by tonight. He'll clean that wound properly and stitch you up right."

"Yeah," Fin said, tenderly lowering his shirt as James went to wash his hands. "That sounds good. Let's hope I'm trail ready before too long. There're places I need to get to, and I don't want to be a burden on you for longer than needs be."

"Your gang has paid me more for board and room than I have made from farming this season, so you're no burden to me. Might as well call this place a halfway house than a farm at this point," James laughed, rubbing Fin's back, getting a smile from the injured man. "But I hear you about wanting to get back on the road to check up on your friends. No worries. The doctor will be over tonight, and we'll get you all mended and have you on your way before long."

Fin made his way tenderly outside and sat by the stream as he waited for James' boy to run to town and fetch the doctor. James came and set him up with some meat and cheese, along with a flask of water as he rested, leaving him to his thoughts as James got back to the endless work he had to do on the farm.

Fin was eternally grateful for the man. He had told Fin of Yozo and Malagar passing through, giving them shelter for a few days before Yozo had packed up and headed back to the Jeenyre Monastery to seek a healing for Malagar who was in worse shape than even Fin. Now James was tending to him...he doubted it would be the last time the farmer was going to give them shelter and tend to their wounded, especially if Reza and Nomad were getting involved with any element of the cult he had uprooted in Rediron.

As he rested, he lazily drifted in and out of thoughts of the mysterious malignant religion that he had pried into. Umbraz stank of the occult. He knew of basic theology, and Umbraz did not number among any devils amongst the Deep Hells. He didn't like that what they faced could possibly be a completely new and unidentified god.

Without having knowledge of the enemy they faced, he felt naked and blind to the hornets nest of danger he had just trampled upon. He had heard a voice in his head, and the priestess' eyes had glowed. Whatever god she worshiped had imbued its followers with some means of supernatural power. The question was, how much power did Umbraz have access to. From his experience with the Lords of the Deep Hells, Umbraz seemed like a fledgling entity, but he worried that, if not dealt with early, the threat could grow out of control.

He tenderly held his side where the priestess had stabbed him with the ceremonial knife. He had beheld the complete devastation a wicked blade could do. The illimoth blade that had stabbed Nomad had almost ended the man in the worst possible way. If *this* ceremonial knife held a similar enchantment upon it....

He waved the heavy thoughts from his mind as he watched the clouds float by, lying at the stream's edge. Dipping fingers in the chilly mountain runoff, he thought back on when he, Nomad, and Reza had been lazily watching a similar canvas of clouds floating by not but a month ago.

He had been less burdened then. He had thought himself a changed man from his old self—from the killer. He realized now that he had not changed that much. When push came to shove, he had no reservations of taking lives that needed to be snuffed out. He had felt nothing more than the adrenalin of the moment and the perfunctory maneuvers of combat while killing the king and the priestess in that chapel. He wondered now if it was ever going to be possible to change that side of himself. He wished so.

The farm boy trotted a horse out along the trail heading into town, waving with a big smile at Fin as he mounted bareback and rode off to fetch the doc. Fin waved back, a smile coming to him. They had somehow found some good folk while out on the trail who really cared about them, even before payment was in the discussion, and he appreciated how special a thing that was. It seemed there were fewer of them around these days....

He lay his head down in the grass, letting the chill air numb his pain a bit, taking the bite off it for the moment. He had been in his head long enough. It was time for a rest. The paths ahead would demand all he had to offer; he instinctively knew. His friends would be counting on him.

He cleared his mind, a smile resting on his pallid face as he drifted off into a long slumber. The trickle of the stream lulled him away into distant dreams, and for the first time in many weeks, he found true rest.

From The Author

We face many struggles throughout our life. Some seem insurmountable. I hope something in these stories provides you with strength to weather your most difficult storms.

I hope you've enjoyed the first book in the Kingdom of Crowns Series! I'm looking forward to finishing the next few books in the series and I hope you're just as excited to read them. It means a lot to me to know that you are here for the journey.

I'm regularly updating my progress and daily routine across my social media platforms. Visit me online for launch dates and other news at:

www.authorpaulyoder.com

tiktok.com (@authorpaulyoder)

instagram.com (author_paul_yoder)

amazon.com

goodreads.com

More Lies Within the Darkness

Fin and Yozo have saved Malagar, but they've only unearthed one piece of the puzzle. Reza and Nomad's investigations reveal how the dark powers have corrupted the region, infecting political and religious offices.

The two quickly find themselves entangled in a web of darkness strung by an unholy god.

With the entire region's might against them, they'll need more than their strength to overcome the cult. But will those with the necessary power be willing to forsake their loyalty for justice?

Continue the adventure in Book 2 of the Kingdom of Crowns trilogy:

Firebrands

Made in United States
North Haven, CT
31 October 2024